SAVE ME

The Donovan Family Series (#7)

MARGARET WATSON

ISBN-13: 978-1-944422-05-9

TITLES BY MARGARET WATSON

The Donovan Family Series
Catch Me (#9)
See Me (#8)
Save Me (#7)
Protect Me (#6)
Cover Me (#5)
Trust Me (#4)
Find Me (#3)
Watch Me (#2)
Love Me (#1)

Into the Storm Series
Family on the Run(#5)
The Dark Side of the Moon(#4)
An Honorable Man (#3)
An Innocent Man (#2)
To Save his Child (#1)

Cameron Utah Series
The Marriage Protection Program (#5)
The Fugitive Bride (#4)
Cowboy with a Badge (#3)
For the Children (#2)
Rodeo Man (#1)

McGinnis Triplets Series
Home at Last (#3)
No Place like Home (#2)
A Place Called Home (#1)

CHAPTER ONE

"Damn that bastard Bennett."

Livvy Marini slammed her office door closed, then tossed the file onto her desk with a little too much force. The manila folder slid across the surface, bumped into the stack of files piled on one side and toppled off the edge. The folder landed in her chair, the contents fluttering to the floor.

Livvy closed her eyes for a long moment and breathed deeply. When she was certain she wouldn't scream with frustration, she gathered the papers and evened them up before replacing them in the folder. Still fuming, she threw herself into her chair and shoved her fingers through her hair. A few strands whispered over her face. Damn it! She'd spent a lot of time on the elaborate French braid that morning.

Sighing, she tucked the hair she'd pulled loose behind her ear, opened the folder and re-assembled it in the correct order. Stared at the picture on the first page.

Anson Bates. Former cop. Arrested a month ago, sitting in jail, awaiting trial. Bates had been charged with four counts of murder, two counts of attempted murder, drug distribution, assaulting a police officer and a whole page of lesser offenses.

Everyone in the State's Attorney's office knew who he was. Bates was a high profile case. National-news high profile.

Bates had been denied bail right after his arrest. But now he had a new lawyer. And Henry Bennett had just petitioned for another bail hearing.

Bennett was the most well-known criminal defense attorney in the city. The most successful.

The most expensive.

Bates' property and money had been impounded – the fruit of his drug crimes. If he was acquitted, he'd get it back. But he couldn't use it for his defense.

So who the hell was paying for Bennett?

More important, how could the SA's office stop Bates from making bail?

This case was a career-maker, and Livvy wanted to be part of it. But since her sister Cilla had been the detective who'd arrested Bates, there was no way Livvy would be in the public eye on this one.

She'd begged to be allowed to do *something*. Her boss had handed her this file, with instructions to get as much information as possible from this witness.

Ryan bleeping Ward.

Bates' partner. A hothead. An adrenaline junkie.

A cop her sister Cilla had arrested for roughing up a suspect.

Yeah, Livvy knew all about Ward, too.

She wondered if Gus knew about her connection to Ward. She shook her head, flopping back in the chair. Of course the Cook County State's Attorney knew about it. Gus Swenson was the ultimate political animal. He knew everything about his assistant SA's, and he'd use Livvy's distaste for Ward to make sure she dug hard into what Bates' partner knew.

And if Livvy didn't want to question Ward? If she still

harbored a grudge for the way Ward had treated her sister? Gus wouldn't give a damn about her tender feelings.

Snorting to herself at the idea of Gus even knowing what tender feelings were, she straightened and picked up the file. Ward had been interrogated by a DEA agent shortly after Bates' arrest. The Chicago P.D. had taken a shot at him, too.

Both organizations had concluded that Ward hadn't known about Bates' criminal activities. Which didn't say a lot about Ward's powers of observation. How had the guy even made detective?

As she read through the file, familiarizing herself with the details of the case and Bates' interrogation, someone rapped on her door. "Come in," she called, glancing up from the file.

The door opened hard, bouncing off the wall. A tall, glowering man stood in the doorway.

He had light brown hair. Gray eyes, and right now they were simmering with anger. They turned stone cold as he studied her. Even his thick, sooty eyelashes didn't soften that glare.

"Can I help you?" she said, setting the file on her desk and closing it, hiding the contents.

"I'm supposed to talk to you." His arms at his sides, he clenched his fists and released. Clenched and released.

Livvy narrowed her eyes and stood up, crossing her arms over her chest. "And you would be…?"

"Ryan Ward. Swenson told me you're investigating Anson. I'm supposed to cooperate with you. Spill my guts." He clenched his fists again as he studied her. "You're Cilla Marini's sister, aren't you? He told me I'd be talking to Ms. Marini, but I figured, what are the odds?"

He stared at her, as if daring her to deny it.

Livvy stared back. "Yes, Mr. Ward, I'm Olivia Marini. Cilla's sister." She watched as he processed the information. His eyes hardened even more. So did his mouth.

Livvy held out her hand, and after studying it for too

long, he finally shook it. His palm was warm, and the calluses on his palms and the pads of his fingers scraped over her skin.

"Have a seat," she said, her back ramrod straight as she curled her fingers into her palms and waited for him to lower himself into one of the chairs in front of her desk.

As he glowered at her, his expression was an open book. He hated being here. He wanted to leave. His jaw worked. His gaze slid toward the door. His foot tapped out a nervous rhythm on the tile floor.

"Why am I talking to *you*?" Ward finally asked.

"Because I'm part of the investigative team for the Anson Bates case," she said, her voice steady. She was in the power position – standing while he sat. She didn't intend to lose her advantage. "Gus Swenson gave me your file. You and I will be working together." She forced herself to uncurl her hand. No way would she let this rude man know he'd rattled her.

"Is this Swenson's idea of a joke?" Ward leaned forward, his gaze as hard as winter ice. "I thought he wanted me to cooperate. Tell you everything I know. So why did he turn me over to *you*, knowing we have history?"

"*We* don't have history, Mr. Ward. What happened between you and Cilla has no bearing on this case." She slid into her chair, holding his gaze.

Ward gripped the arms of the uncomfortable chair. A muscle jumped in his jaw. "Right. You think what happened between your sister and me isn't going to affect how you and I work together?"

Since he was laying it on the table, so would she. "I won't let it. The Anson Bates case has nothing to do with the disagreement between you and Cilla. As long as you cooperate, I can work with you."

"The 'disagreement?' Is that what you call it?" He laughed. The cold, hard sound matched his icy eyes. "Your sister arrested me."

She had no intention of getting into an argument about

what had happened between Ward and her sister. "Cilla's a good cop. She didn't arrest you for fun. Or because it was 'that time of the month.'" She punctuated her words with a vicious slash of air quotes.

"I never said that. Never implied it, either." His face was stone, his eyes hard as granite.

Livvy shrugged one shoulder. "You created the atmosphere. You didn't think one of your buddies would go a step farther? Make a crack like that to Cilla?"

He flinched. Barely, but enough that she noticed. Satisfaction hummed through Livvy. She leaned toward him, her hands pushed flat against her desk. "If someone had said that to me? I would have kicked his ass. Then yours for starting it. And believe me, I'd have enjoyed the hell out of it." Her nails dug into the old, soft wood of the desk. She still got angry every time she thought about what Ward had done. "Regardless, it's in the past, Mr. Ward. Leave it there."

He narrowed his eyes. "So you're just going to forget about what happened?"

"Not at all. But *I* know how to separate my personal life from my professional life, Mr. Ward." She straightened her back, realizing anger was painting her voice with sharp edges. She had to work with this guy. Get him to confide in her. Obvious anger wasn't going to get her what she needed. "Can *you?*"

He shrugged one shoulder. "We'll see, won't we?"

"I guess we will." Livvy swallowed the ball of temper lodged in her throat and pulled the file toward her. "Have you read Mr. Bates's interrogation transcript?"

"I didn't have to read it. I was there."

"I'm not talking about your own interrogation," she said. "I'm talking about Bates'."

"I heard every word Anson said. I was in the observation room during his interrogation." His jaw worked again and he stared out the window behind her, as if fascinated by the vista of rooftops and air conditioning

9

units.

Was Ward pissed off at Bates? Or was he angry he had to cooperate with the SA's office? "It's been a month," she said. "You're a detective. You know witnesses forget details after a few days, let alone four weeks."

He slanted her a glance, but didn't say anything. Didn't have to. The muscles clenching in his jaw told her everything she needed to know.

He needed to read the transcript. Didn't want to admit it.

Savoring her tiny victory over Ryan Ward, she nodded once. "I'll make you a copy so you can review it. Look for anything the prosecutors might have missed. An expression Bates used that has special meaning to him. Some reference that only you would understand. Anything we might not have caught."

Ward rolled his shoulders, drawing her attention to them. His blue dress shirt emphasized how wide they were as it clung to the muscles in his upper arms. "I can recite almost every word of that interrogation in my sleep," he said, shifting his eyes to hers again.

His bleak look told her he probably had, and a tiny breath of sympathy drifted through her. Regardless of what she thought of Ward, it had to be hard to testify against a former partner. Wrenching and painful.

"I don't need a transcript."

"I'll make one anyway. Reading a document is different than listening to someone talk. You might see something." She reached for the folder, opened it and pulled out the transcript. "It can't hurt."

"Fine. I'll read it tonight. Is that all you need from me?" He stood up, and once again filled her small office.

"I'm afraid not," she said, standing as well. He towered over her. "I'll have a lot of questions for you. About where you and Bates went on your shifts, who he talked to, who he ran into more than once. But for starters, read the transcript and mark anything that strikes you as…interesting."

"I want to get this over with," he said.

She raised one eyebrow. "You know you'll have to testify at his trial."

"Anson's a smart guy. He'll take a plea."

"You think so?" Livvy shook her head. "He's had a month to sit in his cell and think about doing serious time. He hasn't budged. Still says he's not taking a deal. Now he's got a new attorney. The best in the city. Bennett is asking for bail again. So why would Bates take a plea and lose his chance to get out of Cook County jail?"

Ward scowled. "What the hell? *Henry Bennett's* his lawyer now?"

"Yes. And he's asking for a bail hearing. Based on the charges against Bates, he shouldn't get it. Bennett must have something up his sleeve." Livvy clenched her teeth and glanced at the picture of the guy on the cover of the file. Bates' smirk made her angry all over again. "My job is to figure out what it is, and how to counter it."

Ward snorted. "Anson knows he won't get bail. He's a master at chess. He has his next five moves planned out."

"Then I'll figure out a way to checkmate him," she said, standing up. "It'll take a couple of minutes to copy the transcript. I'll be right back."

As she edged past his chair, the heat from his body washed over her, carrying his scent. Was he wearing aftershave, or did he always smell like cool fresh air and sunshine?

What the hell? She was wondering about *Ryan Ward's* aftershave?

Clearly, anger at the thought of Bates getting bail had short-circuited her brain. The only thing she should be wondering about was how quickly she could complete her work with Ward.

She absolutely didn't care what he smelled like. Or looked like, for that matter.

He could be the most gorgeous hunk in the history of

hunks. He was off-limits. On top of the ethics issue and the loyalty to her sister issue, what if he was working with Bates?

They were partners. It was possible he'd run back to Bates with information on how the SA's case against him was shaping up.

Her hands weren't quite steady as she set up the copy machine. She braced herself on the machine as she watched the copy spew out. She needed to focus on the case. Keep her head and be careful about what she shared.

Her hands were rock steady as she removed the papers and tapped them on the lid of the copier. Breathing deeply, she headed down the hall toward her office.

When she walked in the door, Ward was holding Bates' file. Thumbing through the contents, he paused to read something.

Rage, accompanied by the bitter taste of déjà vu, roiled her stomach. "What are you doing?" she asked, snatching the folder out of his hand. She held it against her chest and stared at him,

"Doing what you told me to do," he said coolly. "Looking through your notes."

Slamming the folder onto the desk, she stood over him, blood roaring in her ears. "I asked you to look at the *transcript*. Not the entire file."

"Why not?" he asked, leaning back in his chair and letting his gaze drift over her. "You want my help, I need to know everything you know."

"No. You don't." She narrowed her eyes at him. "There's sensitive information in that file. Confidential. Not for general distribution."

The memory of James Dugger, her 'boyfriend,' going through her briefcase a few months ago, looking for his friend's file, made her cringe with shame. The betrayal was still raw. Still fresh.

"I'm cooperating with you, aren't I?" He pushed out of the chair and stood, towering over her. Too close. Staring down at her. "I'm on your side."

She stared right back. Angry witnesses didn't intimidate her. They made her push harder. "Are you?" she asked softly. "When was the last time you saw Bates?"

A shadow flickered in his eyes. "A couple of weeks ago."

"You visited him at Cook County jail."

"No, we had a beer together at the Pipe and Shamrock." His jaw twitched, as if he was grinding his teeth. "Of course I went to Cook County. Only way I was gonna see him."

"What did the two of you talk about?"

His gaze slid to the side. "This and that."

Livvy lifted her chin as she stared at Ward. "Was it something you told him that made him think he could get bail?"

When Ward sucked in a breath, Livvy grabbed the file and slid it into a desk drawer. Didn't look away from him. "He's your partner. Are you going back to the jail and tell him what you saw in his file?" she demanded. *Just like that asshat Dugger planned to do.*

"How're you going to prevent it, Marini? You going to take me into protective custody?" His gaze drifted over her, lingering at her mouth, her breasts, her legs.

A flash of awareness sparked between them, and she sucked in a quick breath. "I'm not interested in babysitting hostile witnesses," she said, although her skin tingled every place his gaze touched. What the hell was wrong with her? Why was she always drawn to the jerks? The guys who wanted something from her?

She took an empty manila folder off the bookshelf, dropped the transcript into it and shoved at him. "Here's the transcript. I'll call you tomorrow."

His fingers curled around the file folder. "My phone number is 773..."

She interrupted, crossing her arms over her chest. "We already have it."

"Of course you do." He lingered for a moment, studying her. "You going to check the logs at the jail? See if I visit

Anson?"

"Will I need to?" She raised one eyebrow and held his gaze.

"What do you think?" he asked, staring back. After a few moments that felt like hours, he stepped into the hall, glancing over his shoulder. "It's been fun, Ms. Marini. I look forward to talking to you tomorrow."

He turned and headed down the hall. Livvy stepped to the door to watch him walk away. To make sure he went right to the reception area. She didn't want him snooping around the office.

It was hard not to appreciate the way he moved. Smooth, flowing steps, no wasted motion. Graceful.

His ass was worth a second look, too.

If she was thinking about Ryan Ward that way.

Which she most emphatically was not.

She stumbled back into her office and closed the door. Where the hell had that come from?

Yeah, he was attractive, with those cool grey eyes, wavy brown hair and that sculpted body. She had a weakness for big guys. So sue her.

But this was *Ryan Ward.* The guy who'd orchestrated her sister's shunning at her police station. The guy who'd made Cilla's life so miserable she'd had to transfer to another district.

The guy *she* was investigating because his partner was a criminal.

She sat heavily in her chair and rubbed at her forehead. As if James Dugger wasn't bad enough, now another loser was ringing her chimes.

Apparently, her string of being attracted to the wrong men continued.

She fumbled for the drawer where she'd stashed the Bates file and pulled it out. Opening it, she tucked the original copy of the transcript where it belonged and began paging through the notes again.

After fifteen minutes, she closed the file. She didn't

remember a thing she'd read.

She glanced at her watch. Six pm.

Time to leave. She'd get some takeout Chinese and work on this at home. She needed to concentrate on this case. Go over all the information in the file and make notes about what to ask Ward tomorrow.

As she stuffed the folder in her briefcase, she glanced at the chair on the other side of the desk. It was horribly uncomfortable, with a broken spring that poked you in the ass if you sat in it. There was no money in the budget for new furniture.

Ward hadn't seemed to mind. He hadn't shifted in his chair, hadn't squirmed. Almost as if he hadn't noticed the broken spring. It spoke to a single-mindedness, a focus, that could be dangerous.

Or seductive. She shivered, remembering the way his gaze had swept over her. Maybe he'd been focusing on…other things.

And maybe she was a complete idiot.

As she slipped on her jacket and headed down the hall, though, an image of Ward appeared in her mind again. Standing at her door, asking if she was going to check the visitor log at Cook County Jail.

Great ass or not, she wasn't going to take anything on faith.

Livvy pulled her phone out of her pocket, googled the number for the jail's visitor office and added it to her contacts.

She'd check with them tomorrow to see if Ward had visited Bates.

CHAPTER TWO

As he turned his Toyota RAV-4 onto Lake Shore Drive, Ryan squeezed the steering wheel until the bumps on the bottom of the plastic dug painfully into his palms. How the hell had he ended up working with Cilla Marini's sister?

Stupid question. That son of a bitch Swenson was pulling another of his damned Machiavellian maneuvers, and his motive was painfully obvious. Swenson was trying to rattle him. Make him lose control. A witness who lost control was a witness who let things spill from his mouth without thinking.

Swenson was counting on Ryan being rattled by Olivia Marini's resemblance to her sister. Thrown off balance enough to lose the filter between his brain and his mouth.

Not going to happen.

He'd been in enough goddamn therapy in the last six months to learn the warning signs for loss of control. Now, he knew how to derail it.

He'd agreed to therapy in exchange for not being charged with battery after Cilla Marini arrested him. He'd hated the idea of spilling his guts to a shrink, had been pissed off about it when he walked into the office.

The therapist he'd been assigned to had actually been helpful. The distraction technique she proposed had been brilliant - attention to the details of his surroundings. As a cop, he did that already. He soaked observations up like a sponge, storing the images, sorting through them to find the odd sock. The thing out of place. Or missing.

That was when he started paying attention to what Mary was saying.

Time to use the tools he'd acquired to focus on something besides Olivia Marini and Gus Swenson.

He glanced in his rear view mirror, cataloging the cars behind him. Rush hour traffic, no one moving too fast, nothing stood out. A cold wind ruffled the lake on his right, sending breakers rolling over themselves and spreading on the sand. A few gulls walked the beach, looking for picnic leftovers. A handful of joggers ran on the path, exercising after work. Business as usual on that side.

Bumper to bumper traffic on his left. People heading downtown for dinner. To see a play. To catch the Blackhawks' game at the United Center.

He scanned the lane on his right for an opening and moved over to exit on Fullerton. He'd grab some takeout from Oscar's. Have a quiet evening at his place.

As he eased into the exit lane, a movement behind him caught his eye. Several vehicles behind his, a car swerved over three lanes and got into the exit lane, as well. As if he'd forgotten he needed to exit and realized it at the last moment.

If he hadn't been focusing on distracting himself from his anger at both Swenson and Bates, along with Olivia Marini, he wouldn't have noticed the quick maneuver of the car. A beat-up Honda Civic. Silver. As close as you could get to an anonymous car in the city.

He kept one eye on the car behind him as he headed for Oscar's. He took the normal route. Didn't try any evasive action. He wanted to see where this was headed.

The silver Honda stayed five cars back. As Ryan turned onto Broadway, he looked for a parking place. When he spotted a car getting ready to pull out, he slowed and turned on his signal.

By the time he'd slotted his SUV into the spot, several vehicles were lined up behind him. The silver Honda was still five cars back.

Ryan lingered in the car as traffic began to move again. The Honda rolled past, but it was hard to see the driver. Male, he thought. Couldn't make out anything else. The window was smeared with dirt. So was the license plate. Either the guy had been traveling on muddy, unpaved roads, or he'd deliberately mucked up the windows and license plates.

His instincts humming, Ryan opened the door and stepped out. If he was a betting man, he'd guess deliberate.

Why was someone following him? He'd just closed a case and hadn't been assigned a new one yet. He had nothing important pending – a few opens, mostly small-time drug cases. And as of today, he was on administrative leave.

Was this about Anson's case?

About his new lawyer's attempt to get bail for that bastard?

He walked into Oscar's, and decided to eat there rather than take his food home. He asked for a table next to the window, and chose a seat with a view of his car. He'd watch and see what developed.

He was half-way through his burger when the silver car with the obscured license plate and windows drove past again. Slowed a little, as if there was traffic ahead of him. The driver glanced toward Oscar's. Then he resumed his careful speed and kept going.

Hmm. Maybe Ryan would stick around and have a beer. See if the guy came by again.

Forty-five minutes later, after stretching one beer as far as he could and no sign of the silver car, he signaled for his check. As he reached for his wallet, the door opened and a group came in. Laughing and talking all at once. Someone was having a good time.

He scribbled his name, stood up and headed toward the door. Stopped.

The group next to the hostess' stand was the Donovan cops. All five of them, including the Fibbie. As he edged past them, the Fibbie gave Ryan the death glare.

Ryan held his gaze. Knocked shoulders as he passed the guy. The Fibbie narrowed his eyes. Too bad. The asshole was blocking the exit. What was Ryan supposed to do? Say 'pretty please, can I get through?'

Ryan pushed through the door into the chilly October weather. As he zipped his jacket, he checked out the Donovans. They were all smiling or laughing. Mia elbowed one of her brothers, then grinned at something he said to her. The lookalikes were talking to Mac. Brendan was on his phone.

They clearly enjoyed each other's company. Had fun together. They looked happy. The way a family *should* look. Last he'd heard, all of them but Mia were dating someone seriously. At least one was engaged.

The five of them were in their own little world. Solid together. When Ryan had walked by, he'd been a momentary distraction. As soon as he was out the door, they'd forgotten him.

He was a guy who passed through their lives like a ghost. A brief flutter of awareness, a momentary pause in their lives. Then nothing.

An outsider.

He'd made Cilla Marini an outsider in the station they'd shared. An invisible person. He'd gotten most of the other cops to shun her. She'd transferred to another district.

He'd been a bastard. No wonder her sister had been so pissed off about having to work with him.

Something burned in his throat, and he swallowed thickly. He had siblings, too. He'd be angry as hell if someone did that to Cammie.

He hadn't talked to his brother or his sister in months. Had no idea what was going on in their lives. Were they happy? Dating? Serious about someone?

Maybe he'd call them. See how they were doing. Reconnect with them.

His therapist had explained that sometimes kids who grew up in abusive homes drifted away from their siblings when they became adults. Trying to forget. To build new lives.

Is that what had happened with him and Cammie and Jesse? Would his family have turned out like the Donovans if they'd been raised differently? Had different parents?

He had no idea. He'd played the hand he'd been dealt and he'd done okay. He was a cop. He loved his job. Yeah, he'd drifted apart from his siblings along the way, but maybe he could repair that bond. Start building a more balanced life that included actual friendships. A real relationship.

Olivia Marini's face drifted into his mind, and he shoved it away. Not her. God, no. He liked party girls. Girls who were all about a good time and nothing more.

Marini was a serious person. Confident. Competent. Good at her job. And hot as a smoking gun.

Exactly the kind of person he'd be interested in if he was looking for a relationship. But she was off limits. After what had happened between him and Marini's sister, that was a closed door.

If she was so pissed off at him, even though he'd apologized to Cilla, she must be close to her sister. Given a choice between him and Cilla? It would be Cilla every time.

Why was he thinking about Olivia Marini, anyway? He had no time for dating, for relationships. Even if he did, he had zero chances with Cilla's sister.

Didn't want any chances with her. Her job as the ASA was to turn him into a rat. Get him to betray his partner, and by extension, every other cop on the force. He'd tell her and her boss Gus Swenson to go screw themselves, but he couldn't do it.

He hadn't realized *his partner* was running a criminal enterprise. Why had he been so blind? So unable to see who Anson really was?

For whatever reason, Ryan had fucked up. Big time. Bates had been selling drugs right under his nose. So Ward would help put his partner away for good.

Maybe that would ease the guilt he felt over his ignorance. His lack of attention to what his partner was doing. Maybe seeing the prison door slam closed on Bates would bring some measure of redemption.

He'd cooperate with Olivia Marini. Didn't mean he had to like it. Anson had committed a lot of crimes, but Marini couldn't make him enjoy crashing through that blue wall of silence.

Dealing with this mess with Bates was the first step. Once he put that behind him, he could straighten out the rest of his life. Fix what was broken in his family. Maybe even find a woman to get involved with. Explore a relationship that was deeper than a puddle of water.

An image of Olivia Marini crept into his mind. Someone like her.

The fact that it wouldn't be Olivia herself caused a pang of regret that was a little harder than it should be.

* * *

Staring at nothing, Ryan sprawled on his coach as the sky lightened outside his window the next morning, rolling a flash drive over and over in his hand. He'd read the transcript the night before, circling several things that didn't sound right. He'd tossed and turned until five a.m., wondering about those details.

Finally, when he hadn't been able to sleep, he'd gotten out of bed and retrieved the flash drive he'd hidden in a box of books on his hall closet shelf.

The night Anson had been arrested, Ryan had bought

the two biggest flash drives he could find. He'd stayed at the station into the early hours and copied all the case files he and his partner had worked together.

The next morning, he'd listened to every word his partner said in the interrogation room. The knowledge that Anson had been able to fool him so completely had burned like acid in his gut. As he'd listened to the solid evidence against his partner, his anger had built. Swelled until it consumed him.

He'd been a fool. A blind, stupid patsy that Anson had played like a virtuoso. It had been mortifying.

So had the bitter truth that his partner had been laughing at him behind his back.

After listening to the whole, painful interrogation, Ryan had deposited one of the flash drives in a safe deposit box. He'd hidden the other in his apartment.

Those two bits of plastic and metal were his insurance. He'd have proof if someone tampered with those files. Anyone with access to the system, or a good hacker, could erase details that might help convict Bates. Add details that might incriminate Ryan.

He curled his fingers around the black plastic fob on his palm. While he'd been downloading the files that night, a tiny voice whispered he was being ridiculous. Paranoid.

He'd copied them anyway.

Listening to Anson's interrogation, Ryan had been damn glad he'd copied them.

Maybe he'd been right to be paranoid. Someone had followed him tonight. Right after he met with an assistant state's attorney.

He opened his palm and looked at the small piece of plastic and metal. Thank God that second flash drive was safely stowed away in a bank vault.

One question had consumed him since the night Anson was arrested. Why hadn't he noticed something was off with Bates? Looking back, his partner had done a lot of things that were innocuous at the time, but suspicious in hindsight. Little things, but little things added up to bigger things.

Maybe his subconscious had noticed something. Why else would he have thought to copy those case files when Anson was arrested?

Ryan had been so stupid. He'd worked with Bates for five years and trusted him completely. Defended him, even to the point of getting arrested. Cilla Marini had found him shoving a hooker up against a wall, questioning her claim that Anson was stealing money and drugs from her.

Ryan uncurled his hand and stared at the flash drive again. Opened his laptop. Turned off his wireless in case someone was cyber-stalking him. Then he plugged in the flash drive.

He'd look at every case he'd worked with Anson. Find the details that would be ammunition against his request for bail, enough that he'd hear the prison door slam shut behind his former partner. In the meantime, he'd continue to visit his former partner in Cook County jail every couple of weeks and pretend he was on Anson's side. Wait for him to spill something important.

When he knew Anson would never see the light of day again, he'd get on with his life. Focus on figuring out why he'd bought Anson's line of bullshit.

Once he did that, he'd make sure it never happened again. He'd been gullible. A total fool to follow Bates so blindly. He'd learned his lesson, though. No one else was going to sneak under his defenses.

From now on, the only person he trusted was himself.

* * *

Ryan pulled into a parking spot at the Garfield Park Conservatory and killed his engine. He was pretty sure no one had followed him this morning. But meeting at this conservatory on the west side of Chicago? Marini must be freaking-out-paranoid about this case. Had someone been following her, too?

She was waiting for him in the gift shop, as she'd promised. When he walked into the small room, he spotted her immediately. She wore tight, dark jeans and a green sweater that looked as if it might slip off one shoulder at any moment. Her hair was loose in a spill of whisky-colored waves over her shoulders.

He swallowed. She'd been attractive yesterday in her conservative dark suit, her hair wound into some kind of intricate braid.

Today, dressed casually, she took his breath away.

She looked up suddenly from the book she'd been examining and met his gaze. Holding it a moment too long, she set the book down and walked over to him. Instead of the power heels she'd worn yesterday, today she wore blue Chucks.

"Mr. Ward," she said, holding out her hand. "Thanks for coming all the way down here."

"Not a problem, Ms. Marini," he said, curling his fingers around hers. Her skin was like silk, and her hand felt tiny and fragile in his. He swallowed once and loosened his grip on her hand when he felt her tug a little. "Interesting choice for a meeting, though."

"Yeah. Sorry." She shrugged, biting her lower lip, and he wanted to lean forward and taste it. "Hope it's not going to make you late for work."

"No." The only work waiting for him was those case files on the flash drive. "Why here, though? Are you that paranoid that someone will overhear us talking?"

She blew out a breath. "Nothing so simple. My sister is looking at wedding venues, and she wanted my opinion on this place. Since I'd already made plans to be out of the office to talk to you, I figured I could talk to Cilla before we met. Two birds with one stone."

"Is your sister still here?" He looked over his shoulder, to make sure he hadn't missed her in the lobby.

"No, she left ten minutes ago." She tilted her head and

studied him. "I told her I was working with you. She shrugged it off. Said you'd apologized to her. That you told her she was right to arrest you." Her lips thinned. "There wouldn't have been a scene if Cilla were still here. She doesn't hold a grudge, Mr. Ward."

"Unlike you," he said, keeping his gaze on her. "You hold a grudge big enough for two people."

"She's my baby sister," Livvy said. "She's always been there for me. Now it's my turn to do something for her."

"Carrying the torch against me?" He raised one eyebrow.

"I'm an attorney. I'm cautious. I don't take anything on faith. Cilla might have forgiven you, but I haven't forgotten what you did to her." She blinked several times. "Cilla loved working at the twenty-second district."

"I already told her I was sorry. That I'd take it back if I could. What more do you want from me?"

"There's nothing I want from you, Mr. Ward." Her eyes were chilly. Her voice was cool. A little distant. "Except information that will help me keep Anson Bates in jail."

He wanted to rip that distance apart. Shake her up. Make her *see* him.

Right now, all she saw was the guy who'd tormented her sister. A guy whose partner was a crook.

He wanted to be more than that. He wanted his self-respect back. He wanted to shed the guilt of being Anson Bates' partner.

He'd have to settle for helping Oliva Marini keep Bates behind bars for a long, long time.

The silence stretched uncomfortably long. Finally, Olivia said, "There's a patio in back of the conservatory. Less chance of being overheard. Do you mind sitting back there, Mr. Ward?"

"Call me Ryan," he said gruffly. "Mr. Ward sounds like my old man."

"Okay," she said after a moment. "I'm Livvy."

"Livvy it is." It suited her, especially dressed as she was

today. Livvy was softer than Olivia. Livvy had fewer hard edges, more fun.

Ten minutes later, they sat at a table on a stone patio, cups of coffee in front of them. Livvy opened a notebook, laid a pen on it, and said, "Did you find anything?"

This was the moment. The turning point. Even though Bates was an asshole, that blue wall of loyalty rose in front of him. Don't snitch on a fellow cop. Keep your mouth shut.

Don't betray a buddy.

But after going over the charges against Bates, reading the transcript and reviewing the files on his computer, he had no choice. Anson had already betrayed him and every one of his fellow officers.

Taking a deep breath, he said, "Yes. I did."

CHAPTER THREE

Livvy picked up her coffee and took a gulp, waiting for the caffeine rush. She needed to be alert for this. Needed to be able to focus. She had to get past what had happened between Ward and her sister Cilla.

She'd talked to Cilla last night. Cilla had confirmed that Ward apologized to her. Cilla had been sure he meant it. She'd accepted his apology and put the whole ugly mess behind her.

It didn't hurt that Cilla was now engaged to Brendan Donovan, the 'best thing that had ever happened to her.' Her sister had other, happier things to focus on.

Now Livvy had to put the nastiness behind her, as well. She had to work with Ward. And if she saw only her sister's tormenter every time she looked at the guy, she wouldn't get anything done.

She glanced around to make sure no one could overhear them. Finally, satisfied that the other two occupied tables were paying no attention, she leaned forward. "What did you find?"

Ward stared at his coffee as if the plain white cup held

all the answers. Finally, pulling something out of his pocket and curling his fingers around it, he lifted his eyes to her. "I found an error in the interrogation transcripts. Anson said we'd arrested a perp recently near a bar in the Morgan Park neighborhood. I know for a fact it wasn't anywhere near the Hole In The Wall. I remembered the case because the arrest was on the block where one of my informants lived.

"So I pulled out my copy of all our case reports from the last five years." He opened his palm to show her a black flash drive, then slid it back into his pocket.

"You kept a copy of all your case files?" she asked, frowning. Why would he have his own copy of official records?

"I have them now."

"Why?"

He looked away, and she followed his gaze to the tall, naked sunflower stalks that filled a field behind the conservatory in the summer. They looked like bones sticking out of the black earth.

Shoving away the morbid thought, she picked up her pen and watched the man across the table from her. Anger and grief warred in his slate gray eyes.

He took a deep breath, as if girding himself for battle. "I made the copies the night Anson was arrested. Why?" He shrugged. "I'm not really sure. I guess, subconsciously, I must have realized something was off with Anson. The next day I listened to both the DEA and our guys interrogate Anson."

He grimaced. "First thing I thought of? Thank God I'd made the copies. It was clear he was guilty. If other cops besides Anson were involved, I was afraid they might try to shift the blame onto my shoulders.

"Second thing? Preserve the evidence. Make sure nothing from our case files went missing. Or got changed."

"That's why I copied the files." He rolled his shoulders and stared into his coffee. "This flash drive, and another one in a safe deposit box, are my insurance policy."

He drummed his fingers on the metal table, and the echo swirled in the crisp fall air. "Last night, after finding that discrepancy in the transcript, I loaded the files onto my computer and looked for anything that didn't line up with what he said in interrogation. I found that address difference. I caught a couple of other addresses that I was pretty sure weren't where we actually put the cuffs on the perp."

"Do you have names? Addresses?" A tingle of excitement rushed through Livvy.

"Yeah." He shoved a piece of paper toward her. She wanted to grab it, but she left it lying there. Let him finish his story.

"Found something else in the files. I didn't have time to review all of them, but there were three recent cases where a suspect we interrogated wasn't mentioned in the report. All in reports Anson wrote up." He shoved a hand through his hair, and clumps of the waves stood up.

Livvy sat up straight, anticipation building. She nodded at him to continue.

"I think these might be important. Maybe more important than the address changes."

His jaw worked as he avoided her gaze. "I should have realized something was going on when Anson volunteered to write more than his share of reports." Shadows filled Ryan's eyes. "Every cop hates writing those things. When he offered, I was grateful. Didn't think twice about it."

"What reason did he give you for doing more than his share of the work?" Livvy asked, gripping her pen hard, ready to make notes.

Ryan lifted one shoulder. "It varied. Sometimes, if a couple of the guys were going for a beer, he'd tell me to take off. Go with them." He swallowed and stared out at the small pond. "Said he was an old fart. Hanging out in cop bars was for younger guys."

He slapped the table and stood up, pacing the small patio. An El train rumbled past the conservatory, the wheels clacking on the tracks. As the noise faded away, he slid back into his chair. Instead of looking at her, he pulled out the flash drive again, stared at it for a moment, then slid it back into his pocket. "Should have known that was bullshit. It's the older guys who spend the most time at the bars. At the time, I just thanked him and took off."

"What other reasons did he give?" She kept her voice steady. Tried to hide her excitement. This could be it. Ward might hold the key to keeping Bates locked up.

Ward closed his eyes and took a deep breath. "He had a million of them. He'd ordered a pizza and it was being delivered to the station. He had plans with his wife and needed to kill some time before she was ready. He needed to check something with another detective and he wasn't back at the station yet. Blah blah blah."

"Those sound like reasonable reasons to stick around," Livvy said as Ward clenched his teeth, his expression tight with anger.

Not at her, she realized with sudden clarity. At Bates. Since Bates was beyond his reach, he was taking it out on her.

His partner had lied to him. Betrayed him. Of course Ward was angry.

Ward hadn't visited Bates since he talked to her yesterday. So that was something. But what had Ward said to Bates when he visited his former partner at Cook County Jail earlier? She wanted to know. Badly. Livvy was almost certain he wouldn't tell her. Since she didn't want to disrupt the flow of the conversation, she scribbled a note to herself to ask him later.

"So tell me about these suspects Bates left out of the report," she said briskly. Time to direct his anger into getting useful information for Bates' prosecution.

"All three of them were drug cases. Lower level guys. We were pressing them for the names of their suppliers. Looking for bigger fish."

"Any idea why he left their names out of the report?" she

asked, scribbling notes in her notebook, trying to hide her eagerness for the information.

He raised one shoulder. "If I'd caught it at the time, I would have figured he just forgot the guys. They weren't helpful, claimed not to know much. But now?" He curled his fingers into a fist on the table. "Maybe the interrogation was all for show. Maybe *Bates* was the bigger fish. Maybe these guys worked for him and he was protecting them."

"If Bates was protecting them, why would he even go see them?"

Ward pulled a piece of paper out of his pocket, opened it and stared at it. "On all three of them, *I* was the one who got their names from a CI. An informant," he added.

"You have names and addresses for the guys he left off the report?" Livvy asked. Her blood pounded in her ears and her chest tightened. Maybe they could get these guys to testify against Bates. Give the judge more reasons to keep him in jail.

"Right here," Ward said, shoving a piece of paper across the table at her. "Along with the arrest locations that were off."

Livvy scribbled their names and addresses. "One of these guys lives not far from here," she said, tapping Freddie Sampson's name with her pen. "I'd like to go and talk to him, as long as we're this close. You up for it?"

Ward tilted his head to study her. "You look like you just won the lottery," he said.

"I did. You gave me information we didn't have." She tapped her foot on the flagstones of the patio. She wanted to jump out of her chair. Question Freddie Sampson. "So let's go. Talk to this guy."

Ward shook his head. "He sees me, he's clamming up. He knows I was Bates' partner. He's not going to open his mouth when I'm around."

"Then I'll go by myself." She shoved her notebook into her bag and stood up. "Thanks, Ward. This is great. I'll let you know what Sampson has to say."

She turned to leave, but Ward clamped his fingers around her wrist. His hand was warm, his skin a little rough. As if he worked with his hands. The calluses on his fingertips rasped against her skin. "Are you crazy, Marini? You can't walk into Freddie Sampson's place by yourself and ask him to rat out Bates. Not the other two, either. These aren't nice guys. You need to take a cop with you." His gaze bored into hers. "Someone from your sister's boyfriend's family."

The message was clear – *someone you trust*.

His finger tightened around her wrist like a cuff. "Better yet, have one of them bring Sampson into their station. Talk to him there."

She looked over her shoulder, her skin sparking where he held her. Trying to ignore the fizzing in her veins, she tugged her hand away from him. She wanted to press her fingers to the spot where he'd held her. Instead, she curled her fingers more tightly around the handle of her bag.

There was no anger in his eyes now. No grief. He actually looked concerned. For her. Not what she expected from Ryan Ward. She blew out a breath. "You're right. I need to show up with some muscle. I'll call Cilla. See who's available."

"Good. Do that."

"Maybe Cilla can go with me."

At the mention of her sister's name, his eyes went cool. "Take one of the men."

She rolled her eyes. "Yeah, she arrested you, Ward. Deal with it. You were roughing up a woman. You deserved it."

"That's not the reason I don't want you to go with your sister. Guys like Freddie Sampson? They don't respect women. You'll get farther if you have a man with you."

Her hackles rose. "This is the twenty-first century, Ward. Women can take care of themselves." She looked him up and down. "But I guess I should have expected you to have that attitude."

"You think I'm a Neanderthal? A knuckle-dragger?"

Antagonism rolled off him in waves as he leaned close. His breath wafted over her, carrying the scent of the coffee he'd been drinking, underlain by a hint of peppermint. "You know nothing about my attitude toward women. Maybe we need to discuss that."

She was angry with Ward. Completely pissed off at his orders to bring a guy with her. So why was she shivering at the way his eyes darkened? Why did his low-voiced, velvety promise make her mouth go dry and her heart thunder against her chest?

"I'd rather talk about the case against Bates." God! Her voice was all breathy. Lower than normal. What the hell was wrong with her?

He straightened, his eyes glittering with something she didn't want to name. "We can do that, too."

"I'll call you after I talk to Sampson," she managed to say. "We'll meet again. Go over what he said."

"You do that."

She nodded once and stepped away from him. "I will. Thank you for these names." She hesitated. They were supposed to be working together. But tension swirled between them, making her reluctant to ask for anything else.

She had to, though. It was her job. "Are you going to keep looking at those cases? See if you can find anything else?"

"What do you think?" He didn't want for her to answer, which was a good thing, because she had no idea what to say. "It's my job right now. I'm on administrative leave while your office works on this bail issue."

"Good. I'll talk to you soon."

"Right." He began walking away, then turned and narrowed his eyes at her. "If you're planning on going to Sampson's place right now, forget it. I'm following you home."

She bristled, irritated he'd read her so well. "If you want to know where I live, why don't you just ask?"

"Don't have to. Already looked you up." He gestured

toward the parking lot. "After you, Marini."

Gritting her teeth, she marched to her car. When she looked in her rear view mirror, he was right behind her in a black SUV. He stayed there all the way to her apartment.

Ward pulled into a parking spot and sat there, his car idling. Waiting for her to go into her building.

Fuming, she slid out of her car and hip-checked the door shut. Unlocked the outer door to her two–flat, walked in and slammed it behind her. When she glanced through the glass, the smug bastard gave her a mocking smile before he drove away.

* * *

The Englewood neighborhood was eerily quiet as Livvy stepped out of Quinn's unmarked cruiser. The steady hum of cars on the busy cross street a few blocks away was background noise, but that was all she heard. No kids played in the front yards. No one walked down the sidewalk. Far down the street, a curtain twitched in an upstairs window. That was the only sign of life.

"This isn't a great neighborhood," Quinn said quietly, standing close to her. "You sure you don't want me to bring Sampson into the station?"

"No. He'll be more comfortable here. More willing to talk, I hope."

Quinn studied her for a long moment, then shrugged. "Your call."

Livvy pressed the doorbell button with more force that necessary to hide the fact that she was a little jittery. When the buzzer sounded, unlocking the door, she jumped back in surprise.

Quinn steadied her with a hand on her arm. "You sure about this?"

"Yes." Livvy straightened her shoulders and took a breath, then opened the door. The staircase up to the first floor was clean, but the wood bore the scars of years of abuse. Innumerable pieces of furniture, trunks, boxes and God knows what else had been hauled up these stairs.

The door on the landing above them opened, and a man stepped into the hall. He frowned when he saw them. "Who are you?"

He'd been expecting someone else. Livvy wondered who it was.

She reached the top of the stairs and held out her hand. "I'm Olivia Marini. This is Detective Quinn. I'm with the state's attorney's office. Would you mind if I asked you some questions about a case I'm working on?"

Sampson narrowed his eyes at her, studying her until she wanted to squirm. Finally he shrugged. "Guess not." A snarling Rottweiler pushed his head through the partially open door behind him. Sampson shoved the animal back with his foot, then pulled the door partially closed. He held onto the doorknob, though. So he could throw the door open any time? Let the dog loose?

Quinn shifted beside her, stationing himself between her and the dog. He rested his hand on the gun at his hip and fixed his gaze on Sampson.

The other man's eyes flicked to Quinn, then back to her. He pulled the door closed. "What do you need?"

"I have a few questions about a case eight months ago." She'd memorized all the details. "Two police officers came to talk to you. Ryan Ward and Anson Bates. Do you remember them?"

When Livvy said 'Bates', Sampson froze for a moment. Then he edged closer to his door. "Hard to remember what happened last month. Eight months ago? Nope."

"Anson Bates was arrested last month for drug offenses, attempted murder and assault. It was a big case," Livvy pressed. "You don't remember that?"

"Radio's broken. Missed the news lately." Sampson tightened his hand on the doorknob.

"So there's nothing you can tell me about what you told Bates that day?"

"Don't know any Bates. Sorry." He fumbled the door open, stepped inside and shut it behind him. The metallic thunk of the locks engaging echoed in the hall.

"Let's go, Livvy," Quinn muttered. He wrapped his hand around her upper arm and urged her down the stairs.

She stumbled down the stairs too fast, with Quinn at her back. The air outside was heavy, as if it was about to storm. Livvy sucked in a deep breath. The narrow hall and steep stairs had carried an old, musty smell.

She stood in front of Sampson's place, scanning the street in front of her. It was still deserted. Almost as if the neighborhood was holding its breath. Waiting for...something.

Movement in a car down the street caught her eye. A man sat behind the wheel, studying the buildings along the block. His gaze passed over her and Quinn, then jerked back.

"Damn it, Livvy." Quinn tugged her toward his car. "Not the time or place to act all touristy."

As Livvy opened the passenger door, she saw a shadow in Sampson's window. He was watching them.

No. Her stomach jumped, then tightened into a hard knot. He wasn't looking at her and Quinn. His attention was focused down the street. On the occupied car.

CHAPTER FOUR

"Quinn." Livvy stared in the side mirror as the car accelerated away from the curb. "Sampson was looking out the window when we left." She watched as the black car followed them onto the street, hating the way her voice quivered. "Not at us. I think he was looking at the guy in the black car behind us."

Quinn turned his head sharply to stare into the rearview mirror. "I can't make him out. Did you get a good look at him?"

"Male. That's all."

"Don't turn around," Quinn ordered. "Let's see if he follows us."

Livvy's grip tightened on the seat. She stared into the side mirror, leaning forward to keep the black car in view.

"Can you tell what kind of car it is?" Quinn asked.

"Nope." Black was as much as she could give him. "It has a matte finish on the hood. Other than that, if you need more car information, you've got the wrong sister."

Quinn shook his head. "Too bad Cilla didn't educate you."

He was trying to lighten things up. She appreciated that. But Livvy couldn't tear her gaze away from the car behind them.

They turned onto a busier street, and she lost sight of their tail. Quinn glanced in the rear view mirror too often as he drove. When he eased into the traffic on Lake Shore Drive, Livvy loosened her grip on the armrest. "Is he still following us?"

"Can't see him, but he could be behind us. Hard to tell with this much traffic." He glanced at Livvy out of the corner of his eye. "You said you needed to talk to three guys. We'll bring the next one into the closest station."

"Connor said he'd go with me tomorrow." Her gaze darted to the side mirror. The black car wasn't there.

"Trust me, Livvy. Connor isn't taking you to the next guy's house. Not after I tell him about our visit today."

"Maybe it was a coincidence. That the guy pulled out at the same time we did."

"Yeah. Maybe it was. Maybe not." He glanced at her. "I'm calling everyone else. No one's taking you to the next guy's house, Livvy. Deal with it."

She was crazy about the Donovans, but this was the downside of the close knit family. They stuck together like burrs on a shoelace. If Quinn told them not to take her on more visits, not one of them would do it.

She didn't want to need them. She hated feeling weak. Not in control. After today, though, she knew she couldn't go alone. And Quinn was probably right. Going to the next guy's house, even with an escort, might not be the smartest move.

She turned in her seat and studied the traffic behind her. Far behind them, she caught a glimpse of a black car with the same matte finish on the hood as the car that followed them from Freddie Sampson's.

"He's still behind us."

"He's not going to follow us into the station, Liv," Quinn said, focusing on the traffic ahead of them. "No way for him to figure out who you are. But I'll make sure I lose him before we get there."

Quinn cut across traffic suddenly and veered onto an exit ramp. Livvy turned and watched behind them for a long time, but she didn't see the black car again.

She took a deep, shuddering breath. Yeah, maybe she wouldn't argue with Connor about bringing the next guy into the station tomorrow.

* * *

Ryan sprawled on his couch, his feet up on the ottoman, as he read through another case file. After meeting Marini, he'd spent the rest of the day with the files, and was about half-way through them.

He swallowed the last bite of pizza and took a gulp of Goose 312 as he jotted down a note on his yellow pad. A lot of people he and Bates had talked to in the past year hadn't made it into the reports. Why hadn't he caught that?

Because he'd been blinded by his trust for the man who'd become the closest thing he'd had to a father figure.

Bates had seen that need in him. Used it to camouflage his crimes.

God damn it, Anson. Why didn't I see what a bastard you were?

What had *he* been thinking? How could he have missed all the signs? Yeah, Anson was careful, but Ryan had been pretty damn sloppy.

He hadn't checked the reports after Anson wrote them up. Why would he? Anson was older than Ryan, had more experience. He knew how to write a report.

He'd believed Bates' explanation when they'd gone somewhere unexpected, or followed a different trail in an investigation. Ryan had trusted Bates completely.

Ryan had had his head up his ass.

No more. He'd made a big mistake, but he was going to help fix it. He'd make sure Marini checked all the people who'd been left out of his reports. It would keep them busy.

Working together.

The wind had lifted strands of her hair off her shoulders that morning, as they sat on the patio at Garfield Park Conservatory. She'd tucked them behind her ear absent-mindedly as they'd talked, and his fingers had itched to do it for her. To slide his fingers through those wavy strands, see if they were as soft as they looked.

See if her mouth was as soft as it looked.

He was out of his mind.

He didn't even *like* Marini.

Right?

He reached for his phone without thinking and pressed her contact. It rang three times before she answered. "Marini."

"It's me. Ryan Ward," he added, feeling like an idiot. *It's me* was the kind of thing you said to your girlfriend. Or a close buddy. Someone who'd recognize your voice.

"Hey, Ward," she said. She sounded breathless.

"Did I interrupt something?" he asked, his mind going places it shouldn't.

"Just out for a run." The wind howled through her phone, crackling and whistling. "What's up?"

"I found more names omitted from reports," he said, shame closing his throat. He cleared it once. "I've gone back two years."

The static-y noise stopped. She must have moved into a doorway. Or somewhere sheltered from the wind. Cupped her hand over her phone to hear him better. "You think this has gone on for a while?" Her voice was sharp. Excited. Like he'd just given her a gift.

He hesitated, that instinct to protect a partner rising up again. Then he forced himself to continue. "Maybe. Probably." He looked down at the list of names he'd written. "Follows the same pattern as the first three. Drug cases. Low level guys. Maybe he was planning to recruit them? I have no idea, but it's a pattern."

"I talked to Freddie Sampson today," she said. The wind

began howling again. She must have started walking. "And before you ask, no. Not by myself. One of Brendan's brothers went with me."

"Get any information?"

There was a long pause. "Maybe." She cleared her throat. "Spooky neighborhood. Deserted. Sampson was home, though."

He heard her swallow through the phone. Shot up in his chair. "What happened?" His voice was sharper than he'd intended. Because she'd been an idiot to go there. Not because he was scared for her.

"Nothing happened." She swallowed again. "Quinn was with me. Sampson clammed up as soon as I mentioned Bates. We got nothing from him. But there was a guy in a car on the street."

Thank God he'd made her take a cop with her. Her breath stuttered, and he gripped the phone more tightly. "Was it a silver car? Dirty?"

"No, it was black." Her breath huffed out. "The hood had a matte finish. All I could tell about the driver was that he was male."

"And?" There was more to the story. Or she wouldn't be breathing so hard. Swallowing so much.

"He followed us. Onto the Drive. There was a lot of traffic. We didn't see him follow us off."

'But he might have' hung in the air, taut as a bowstring. He could practically smell her fear wafting through the phone.

"Where did Donovan drop you off?" he asked, careful to keep his voice casual.

"At his station. I left my car there."

Thank God. If the guy had followed them, seeing Donovan pull into a police lot should have scared him off.

"Donovan brings the next guy into his station," he said, his voice gruff.

"He already told me that. And I agreed." The wind began whistling through her phone. She'd started running again.

"Okay. Maybe the Donovans are good for something after all." He heard the sound of feet hitting the pavement approaching Livvy, then fading away. "Where are you running?"

"The lakefront path. Nice views, no traffic to worry about, people around."

"That silver car I mentioned?" Ryan clenched his phone more tightly. "He followed me yesterday. After I left your office. You need to watch your six, Livvy.

"And what kind of an idiot are you, anyway? Someone followed you today, and you're out running on the lakefront path?"

Silence. "You're kind of freaking me out, Ward," she finally said. "It's only seven p.m., but it's dark as an elephant's butt hole out here."

"Then maybe you should do your running at a gym." She'd be safer there than on a dark path along the lake.

"Don't belong to one."

"What?" Time to dial it down before he'd completely unnerved her. "Can't afford it on the huge salary Swenson pays you?"

"You got it." Her voice had lightened. "I spend that pile of money on fancy clothes and expensive shoes. Extravagant meals at swanky restaurants."

"I can tell. I liked those fancy shoes you wore today." Were they *flirting?* God, no. He was trying to distract her.

"Nothing like a good pair of Chucks." He heard her breathing. It was a little ragged. Rougher than usual.

Because she was running, you jerk.

"I'll take your word for it," he said, taking another pull from his beer. "I'm not into that hipster stuff."

"Ha! Trying to shame me? Not going to work. I wore Chucks long before the hipsters claimed them."

"That put me in my place." He swallowed. Yeah, they were flirting. *So* not a good idea. Even if he was just trying to take her mind off the black car that had followed her.

"You carrying pepper spray?" he asked.

"Of course. I always do."

"How old is the canister you have?"

"No idea. I've had it for a while. Never had to use it."

"You need a new one." His mind flooded with images of her trying to use outdated pepper spray on an attacker. Some pissed-off guy would knock it away from her. Then knock..."I'll get one for you. I know the reliable brands."

"I can pick it up myself," she said. "Just tell me what to get."

He'd bet a million bucks she wouldn't get a new one. "No. I'm going to put it into your hand so I know you have it. I'll meet you at your office tomorrow."

"I won't be there," she said. The wind wasn't blowing as hard through her phone. "I'm out of the office. Investigating. Maybe the next guy on the list will have something to say."

You can investigate the hell out of me.

She grunted once, as if she'd bent over.

"You okay, Marini?"

"Yeah. Just got home. Stretching."

Thank God he'd kept her on the phone long enough to make sure she was safe. "Where are you meeting your Donovan escort tomorrow?"

"Connor's station. The twenty-third."

"What time are you supposed to be there?"

"Ten."

"I'll meet you there at nine-thirty with the pepper spray." He'd slide in and out before any confrontations with a Donovan.

She paused for a split second. "Fine. See you tomorrow, Ward."

His phone went dead. Maybe she was having second thoughts about the flirting, too.

He set the phone down on the table next to the couch and took another drink of beer. He should be kicking himself for starting the flirting.

Instead, anticipation rolled through him in a heavy wave. He tried to tamp it down, but it lingered as he finished his beer.

Hung around long after he'd fallen asleep, in the form of sexy dreams about Livvy Marini.

CHAPTER FIVE

Livvy wrapped her fingers around the paper coffee cup and let it warm her fingers as she stepped into the twenty-third district station. It was cold for November in Chicago, and she'd forgotten her gloves. She'd been too focused on getting here. On meeting Connor and finding Jerry Williams.

She rolled her eyes. Yeah, she wanted to talk to Williams, but that's not why she'd run out the door like her pants were on fire. She wanted to see Ryan. *Ward.* Get the pepper spray, and talk about what else he'd found.

Recognizing her from yesterday, the desk sergeant looked up as cold air rushed into the warm lobby. He nodded. "Detective Donovan isn't here yet. Have a seat." He jerked his head toward the uncomfortable plastic chairs that lined the wall.

"I'm meeting Detective Ward first," she said. "From the twenty-second district. Is there somewhere private we could talk?"

The desk sergeant studied her for an uncomfortably long moment. Did he think it was more than a business meeting?

Squaring her shoulders, she stared back at him. She didn't care what he thought.

"Conference room upstairs," the sergeant finally said. "You can use that."

As she lowered herself into the slippery, rigid chair, Ward's telephone conversation from the night before replayed itself in her head.

Not for the first time.

She thought he'd been flirting with her. Had she been flirting back?

She didn't even like Ryan Ward. She was pretty sure he didn't like her. But their conversation last night? She sighed. If it walked like a duck and squawked like a duck...yeah. They'd been flirting.

She'd be all business today.

The door opened with another whoosh of cold air, and she looked up to see Ward walk into the station, coffee cup in his hand. Light blue. Letter D that looked like the @ symbol. He'd gotten his coffee from Della's. Just like she did.

"Hey, Sarge," he said with a smile to the man behind the desk. "I'm Ryan Ward. From the twenty-second."

Livvy was shocked at the way Ryan's smile transformed his face. That smile made him...approachable. Likeable. Damn attractive. The kind of guy a single woman might want to get to know better.

"Right," the sergeant said. "Someone here for you. Behind you," he added, nodding at Livvy. "Told her you could use the conference room upstairs."

"Thanks, Sarge," Ward said. He turned around and spotted her. "Hey, Marini."

Something flickered in his eyes, but it was gone before Livvy could interpret it.

He hadn't smiled at her, though.

Calling herself every kind of fool, Livvy stood up and tried to look in control. Unaffected by his smile. "Hey yourself, Ward."

She must not have succeeded. Ward's shoulders relaxed, his mouth softening. "Let's go upstairs."

Livvy felt his gaze on her back as she walked up the stairs. It sent a shiver down her spine that she tried to ignore.

When they reached the conference room, he pulled out a chair for her. Waited for her to sit, then slid into the one on the end of the table. If she moved, her knees would brush against his.

Taking a deep breath, Livvy allowed herself to study Ward. His eyes were more unguarded than yesterday. Or the day before.

God! Had he seen something besides professional interest in her gaze? Had sappy, too-interested Livvy made an appearance in the few seconds before she'd managed to slap on her impenetrable lawyer face?

"Give me a minute," he said, lifting his coffee and gulping the hot liquid. He closed his eyes, as if savoring every last molecule of caffeine.

"Late night last night?" she asked, watching as he downed another mouthful.

Oh, God. What was wrong with her?

Had she really asked him, in a roundabout way, if he'd had a date?

Setting the coffee carefully on the wooden table, he wrapped his fingers around the paper cup. As if, like her, he needed to warm his hands. "Yeah. It was. After we talked, I finished going through our old cases. All the way back to the beginning."

"Anything more?" She leaned closer across the table, stupidly relieved he'd been working instead of...Yeah. Not going there.

"Same stuff. Names omitted." He took a deep breath. "It went back three years. Before that? Nothing."

"What was going on right before it started?" she asked, gripping the cardboard cup hard and trying to keep the excitement out of her voice. "Did something change in his personal life? His professional life?"

Ward's mouth tightened. "Nothing that would turn him into a crook. There was no tragic story of his wife or kids getting sick. No elderly parents who needed expensive, specialized care. No urgent need for cash. At least that I knew of."

"Would you have been able to tell if there was something? Even if he'd been trying to hide it?"

His fingers curled into a fist. Her gaze dropped to his hand, and he slid it off the table. "Partners spend eight or nine hours a day together. Sometimes more." His voice was flat. As if he'd locked that part of himself so far inside that it would never see the light of day again. "When we're in the car, we talk. A lot of the guys I know? They're closer to their partners than their wives. So, yeah. Anson might not have told me if he had personal problems, but I think I would have known something was off."

Livvy frowned. "How can a guy who was a good cop suddenly turn into a crook? There must have been a trigger."

"Yeah. Seems like there should have been." He shoved his fingers through his hair, and her gaze followed its trail. "I've been thinking about it since he was arrested, but I can't come up with a damn thing."

He scowled into his coffee cup, as if the answers could be found in the dark brown depths. "Maybe it was nothing more complicated than seeing the dealers making handfuls of money and wanting a piece of it. I don't know, Livvy. I have no idea what made him turn."

He'd called her Livvy. Not Marini. She swallowed as warmth slid through her. "You must have noticed something different," she said softly.

He looked up at her again, and the combination of anger and sadness in his eyes made her want to reach across the table to him. She pressed her fingers hard to the table instead. "I want to know as badly as you do. I want to know why I didn't see it coming. How I missed all the signs. Trust

48

me. If I knew, I'd tell you."

"I believe you," she said. "I do. I just hoped that...that..."

"That an explanation might help us find more information," he finished. "Yeah. Not going to happen."

She stared at white knuckles and relaxed her hands, then took a deep breath. "Okay. Then we'll work with what we have."

"Right." He glanced at his watch and his mouth thinned. "I'll give you the names later. I'm gonna take off. Your Donovan buddy will be waiting for you." He reached into his pocket and pulled out a vial of pepper spray. "This is brand new. Strongest available."

He dropped it into her palm, and his fingers brushed her skin. The sensation raced up her arm.

He leaned closer, his blue eyes intense. "It will disable any attacker. And if you're going to run alone, you might need it."

"Are you trying to scare me?" She sat up straight, trying to hide her fear. She refused to show any weakness.

"Absolutely. Did I succeed?"

She swallowed once. Again. "I'd be an idiot if I said no," she muttered.

"Thank God you're not an idiot." He studied her for a long moment. "That running you do along the lakefront? Don't do it alone anymore," he finally said. "Get someone to go with you. Your boyfriend. Another friend. Someone from your neighborhood. There are too many places to hide along that lake shore path."

"No boyfriend. No friends who run with me. I like to run alone." As soon as the words were out of her mouth, she kicked herself. Why had she told him she didn't have a boyfriend? Why hadn't she left it at 'I like to run alone'?

He'd shaken her. Scared her. She didn't think before she spoke.

Those were the only reasons.

Right.

"Alone might not be smart right now, Marini."

He'd called her Livvy a few minutes ago. "I have brand new pepper spray." She wiggled the canister. "I'll be fine."

One side of his mouth curled up. "You said you'd never used that stuff."

"No. Thank God."

"Make sure you're downwind so you don't spray yourself. Kind of hard to fight off an attacker if you're wheezing, coughing and crying."

"Wow." She opened her eyes wide. "I never thought of that. *Don't spray yourself.* You're a genius, Ward."

"Yeah, go ahead and make fun." One side of his mouth twitched. "Just don't expect me to flush out your eyes and wipe the snot off your face when you get blasted by your own pepper."

The picture he painted was shockingly intimate – Ward holding her hair back. Rinsing off her face with warm water. Handing her tissues to wipe away the mucous and tears.

Because the images stirred a yearning that buzzed through her like fire, she retorted, "Don't worry. I'll call a friend if I need help in the personal care department."

The softness in his expression vanished. The smile disappeared from his eyes. Once again, he was the closed off, guarded man who'd stormed into her office. "Glad to know you have it covered, Marini."

He shoved away from the table. "You gonna call me tomorrow? Tell me what Jerry Williams had to say?"

"I will," she said. She drank the last of her cold, bitter coffee. "I'll call tomorrow evening." She couldn't resist adding, "After my run."

He stared at her for a long moment, then nodded. "Talk to you tomorrow night."

* * *

Livvy's gaze swept the street in front of her as she ran. Back and forth from cars to trees to the recessed doorways of houses and apartments. She'd been jumpy since she'd walked out of her apartment three blocks back.

Every swaying shadow made her falter. Every rustle of a small animal in the leaves on the ground made her jump. She'd cataloged every car parked along the street, looking for a small black car.

A block before she reached Lake Shore Drive, she spotted a man sitting in a black car parked at the curb. A Toyota, she was pretty sure. A small one. The driver didn't look up as she ran past, but a chill ran down her spine.

Matte hood. Not glossy.

She glanced over her shoulder and saw the Toyota pulling away from the curb. She ran a little faster.

When she reached the ramp to the tunnel, she turned and ran backward for a moment. Her shoulders relaxed when the black car turned the other way. She watched until he disappeared from sight.

After one final sweep, seeing no one else, she turned and headed down the sloping ramp.

She'd always thought the green lights illuminating the tunnel were quirky. A charming throwback to the previous century. Tonight, they cast eerie, quivering shadows on the graffiti-covered walls. The flickering green looked ominous. Threatening.

She took a deep breath and ran a little faster. Burst onto the ramp on the other side as if she'd been shot out of a gun.

She slowed at the top and studied the almost empty parking lot on Recreation Drive. A couple ran on the adjoining path, far to her right, heading toward the Loop. Another man jogged equally far away on her left. Heading her way.

No one else.

She swallowed the copper tang of dread and jogged over toward the path. She turned right, heading toward downtown. There would be more people that way. There always were, the closer you got to the Loop.

It was cold tonight, with a sharp, biting wind off the lake.

It made her ears burn and her nose numb. She pulled the sleeves of her running jacket over her fists, clutching a fold of fabric. No wonder no one was running tonight.

She could be at home, watching television or reading the book she'd started a few nights ago. But no. She was out in the cold, deserted night, being a stubborn idiot. Refusing to let Ryan Ward scare her away from her favorite running path.

In the distance, she heard the faint sound of feet behind her. Had to be the man she'd noticed before she got on the path. As she ran along, she felt some of her anxiety melting away. The rhythmic sound of the waves slapping the sand far ahead of her soothed her. So did the crash of whitecaps breaking over the rocks to her left.

As the rocks transitioned into sand, she heard the footsteps again. Closer.

The couple in front of her were two shadows in the distance. They'd never hear her scream over the roar of the lake.

Picking up the pace, she glanced over her shoulder. The man was alarmingly close. A dark hoodie cast his entire face in shadow. His dark pants blended with the night. His light shoes only emphasized how dark the night was next to the lake.

His mouth opened. He was calling to her. She stumbled over a rock on the path and flailed for a moment as a sharp pain stabbed through the sole of her foot. She hopped on one foot until she recovered her balance. Ignoring the pain in her foot, she began sprinting.

She ran flat out, searching frantically for a place to hide. But there was nothing but sand, rocks and water. No crannies to curl herself into. No buildings with warm, welcoming lights.

Just the path, unspooling into the darkness.

He was closer. His feet slapped the ground behind her, the sound now audible over the noise from the restless lake.

Her hands shook as she tried to unzip her pocket. The

zipper caught on the fabric. Refused to move. She shoved two fingers through the tiny opening. Barely grabbed the canister of pepper spray. Why hadn't she kept the stupid thing in her hand? What good was it going to do in her damn pocket?

She almost had the slippery vial in her palm when her fingers, wet with sweat even in the cold air, lost their grasp. The pepper spray fell to the asphalt and rolled into the grass at the edge of the path.

Livvy reached for it as she ran. Missed. The man was almost on top of her. She stopped. Wrapped her fingers around the spray. Picked it up. Whirled to face him, her arm extended. Her finger trembled on the trigger, waiting for him to get close enough.

Her finger was pressing on the trigger, ready to release a stream into his face, when he reached out and snatched the vial from her hand.

CHAPTER SIX

"What the hell is wrong with you, Marini?" Ryan Ward scraped the hood away from his face and glowered at her. "Shoving pepper spray in my face?"

Livvy sagged against a tree next to the path, her shaking legs unable to hold her weight. "Ward?" Trembling, she stared at his scowling face. "Why were you chasing me?" Rough bark dug into her back. Her heart thundered in her chest, so loud in her ears she was sure Ward could hear it.

Resting her hands on her knees, she bent over to ease the stitch in her side. Her breath sawed in and out, the cold air burning her lungs.

She felt him towering over her. Too close. The scent of his aftershave and the wild, misty smell of the lake surrounded her, mixed with the tang of clean sweat.

His fists were at her eye level. One of them clutched her vial of pepper spray. His own ragged breathing sent puffs of condensation into the air.

She closed her eyes, blocking out the sight of Ward. Her pepper spray, so useless when she'd needed it.

She'd been defenseless. If he had been someone who

wanted to hurt her, she would have been completely at his mercy.

Oh, she'd have tried to fend him off. She'd have kicked. Scratched. Screamed. Tried to knee him in the balls. But he was so much bigger than her. So much stronger. He would have squashed her like a mosquito.

Her throat closed and tears trickled down her face. Mortified, she sank to the ground, buried her head in her knees. The cold from the dirt seeped into her bones and the fabric of her running pants slowly dampened with her tears.

Ward's running shoes gleamed in the darkness. He stood in front of her, completely motionless. Why wouldn't he leave?

"Go away," she said, her voice thick. "Keep running."

He squatted in front of her. "Marini."

She held her breath, hoping he'd stand up again. Leave her alone with her tears.

"Livvy." His voice shivered over her as his hand dusted her shoulder, fingertips skimming the fabric of her jacket. As if he expected her to shrug him off.

Yesterday, she would have. Today, she let out a wobbly sigh. "You scared me," she whispered.

"I know. I'm sorry." His hand settled on her shoulder. Warm. Heavy. Comforting.

Wiping her wet cheeks on her legs, she lifted her head. His breath fluttered over her face and lifted the fine strands of hair at her temple. He tucked them behind her ear with a hand that shook.

"Can you stand up?"

She swallowed the snarky words that formed in her mouth. They stuck to the lump in her throat, making it bigger. Suffocating her.

Ward took his hand off her shoulder, and she wanted it back. She opened her mouth to ask him to touch her again. Bit off the words before they could escape.

He gripped her upper arms with both hands and pulled

her to her feet. She swayed a little, and he cautiously folded her against him. Wrapped his arms around her and held her lightly. Careful not to press.

She would never have imagined Ryan Ward could be gentle. So comforting. But the pressure of his arms on her back was reassuring. Calming. As if he'd protect her from the world. She burrowed into him like a small animal searching for shelter.

Her head fit perfectly into the hollow between his shoulder and his neck, and she inhaled the drying sweat and gingery soap scent of his skin. The faint aroma of fabric softener wafted up from his clothes.

Ordinary, mundane smells. Everyday smells. Somehow, they settled her. Along with the weight of his arms tightening around her. Holding her solidly against him.

Finally, after they'd stood pressed together at the side of the path for way too long, she eased away from him. For a split second his arms tightened around her, as if he didn't want to let her go.

The next moment he stood two feet away. Out of her reach.

"I wasn't running away from *you*." Her voice was scratchy with tears, but she forced the words out. It was important he realize that. "I couldn't see who was chasing me. The hoodie hid your face."

"I figured that out when I got close enough to see your expression. I know you're not a big fan, but I didn't think I'd terrify you." He tried to smile but it slid away. He turned his head, as if checking the path. "Think you can walk home?"

She drew in a deep, shuddering breath. Time to pull herself together. "Of course I can walk home. Now that some goon isn't chasing me."

The goon's shoulders relaxed. Not completely. But enough to reassure her that Ward knew she was kidding.

"Okay. Let's go."

* * *

Ryan walked beside Livvy, glancing at her every few seconds. She'd stopped crying, but the streaks of dried tears on her face were silvery in the moonlight.

What kind of an idiot chased a woman on a deserted running path? When she couldn't see him clearly?

The kind who'd been terrified of who *else* might be waiting for her along that path. His intentions had been good, but he deserved to have his ass kicked into the middle of next week.

He shoved his hands into his pockets and found the smooth cylinder of pepper spray he'd taken from her. God! She hadn't even been able to get the damn stuff out of her pocket tonight. If he'd been someone intent on hurting her, she would have been toast.

Clamping the vial in his fist so tight it made his palm hurt, he pulled it out and shoved it at her. "Next time you're running, keep it in your hand."

She took it from him, her fingers cold where they brushed his palm. She stared at the small cylinder as they walked, turning it over and over in her hand. Then she slipped it into her pocket. "Don't think I'll be running at night for a while."

"I don't care when you run. Make sure it's in your hand. It doesn't do squat in your pocket."

"Yeah." She tried to smile, but her mouth trembled. "I already figured that out."

Guilt washed over him in a shuddering wave. "Look, Marini, I'm so…"

"Stop," she said, slapping her hand over his mouth.

They stumbled to a halt and stared at one another for a long moment. Her gaze held his, and he wanted to press his mouth to her palm. Taste her.

Before he could act on his reckless, dangerous impulse, she dropped her hand and stepped back. "You've already apologized," she finally said. "Let's get away from here before we talk."

She shivered, and he realized she was cold. "You want my jacket?" he asked.

She stumbled to a halt. "You're offering me your jacket?"

He rolled his shoulders, shamed by the surprise in her eyes. Why wouldn't she be shocked at his offer? He'd been a total asshole to her. "You're cold."

"Thank you," she said. Her voice trembled, but it was soft with gratitude. With another emotion he wouldn't name. She touched his arm. "That's very sweet of you, but I can't take your jacket. You'd be really cold if I did."

"I can handle it." He cleared his throat, ashamed all over again by the wobble in her voice. "You don't have much meat on your bones."

"I'm tougher than I look."

Yeah, she had been. Until he'd scared the crap out of her.

"How about we share it?" he said, shrugging one arm out of its sleeve. He wrapped the soft, worn material around her shoulders, pulling her tight against his body. "That better?"

Livvy curled her fingers into the fabric as she leaned against him. "Yes. Thank you." The quiet whisper of her voice floated up to him. Her body continued to tremble, though. He wrapped his arm around her waist and pulled her closer. Now she was plastered against him from hip to shoulder.

Her shivering slowed, then stopped. By the time they reached Waveland Avenue, all the tension had drained from her body. She huddled against him as if they walked together like this all the time.

Holding her as she'd regained her balance had affected him more than he'd expected. The moment had been tender. Powerful. Amazing. And he'd wanted to keep holding her.

Now, as she relaxed into him, the sensation of her fit,

slender body tucked into his side roused all his protective instincts. Seeing such a strong woman fall apart had shaken him. Shocked him.

He drew her closer to his side.

She melted into him.

He could have walked with her snuggled against him forever. But when they reached the sidewalk on Waveland and walked past the New York building on their left, she slowed, then stopped.

Her fingers whitened on his jacket, and she stared at the skyscraper.

She shifted to look at him, still pressed against his side. The soft weight of her breasts brushed against him, making every muscle in his body tense.

Some more than others.

"I used to live there," she said, nodding at the tall building. "I moved a month ago. Haven't gotten around to changing the address on my driver's license."

It was hard to think with all his blood rushing south. "What are you saying?"

She gripped his tee shirt in her fist. Her knuckles brushed against his abdomen, and he had to stifle a groan. "If I still lived there, I wouldn't have seen the car parked on Waveland. The same car that followed us away from Freddie Sampson's place. I would have walked down the driveway in front of the building right to the underpass. But the guy in the car would have seen *me*."

The haze of lust vanished as if he'd been drenched with ice water. His arm tightened around her and he pulled her closer. "That same black car was parked on Waveland? You walked right past it?"

She nodded, staring at the darkened street beside the high rise. "What if it had been him chasing me instead of you?" she whispered. Her breath shuddered out as she studied the dark street next to the high rise.

"Don't think about it," he said. "It wasn't him."

The possibility made ice form in his veins. What if he

hadn't been out there tonight, waiting for her? "So far, all they've done is watch."

"They?" Her voice sharpened.

"I told you about the silver car that followed me when I left your office the other day. Honda Civic." He swallowed, wondering if it had followed Livvy, as well. "Haven't seen him since, though."

"Did you run the plate? Find out who it was?"

"No." He hugged her close as they began walking again. "The license plate was smeared with mud. Couldn't read it."

She was silent until they rounded the corner of her street. "This is getting creepy," she said, gripping his shirt more tightly. She hadn't let go of him since they started walking again.

She could hold onto him for as long as she wanted.

"Yeah," he said when he realized she was waiting for him to respond. "Looks like talking to Freddie Sampson opened a can of worms."

"And Jerry Williams, too," she added.

"He have anything to say today?"

"Not a word." When she shook her head, a few strands of hair got loose and scraped across his face. They caught in his scruff, wrapped around his face and clung. He let them linger for a moment before brushing them away. "As soon as he heard Bates' name, he stood up and walked out of the room."

"Are you talking to Carl Philby tomorrow?" His was the third name he'd given her.

"Yeah. Brendan's bringing him in."

"Maybe you'll get something out of him. Carl has always been easy to pressure. Threaten him with some jail time, and he'll fold like a house of cards. Tell you what he knows."

"I'll give it a try. I'll wear my power suit." The smile in her voice made him press his fingers into her waist. The muscles of her belly jumped beneath his hand, and she sucked in a breath.

Maybe he wasn't the only one enjoying this closeness.

She slowed as they reached an older brick two flat. She fumbled for her keys in a tiny pocket hidden in the waistband of her running pants. A flash of pale skin at her abdomen, quickly hidden as she dropped her shirt, made him swallow as she opened the outer door and fumbled with the lock on the inner one. When he didn't join her, she turned and frowned at him.

"What's wrong?"

"I wasn't sure you'd want me to come in," he said, feeling like an idiot when she grabbed his shirt again and yanked him over the threshold.

"Of course I want you to come in," she said.

She said it as if only an idiot would think otherwise. So he edged close in the tiny lobby.

The silence was loud as she unlocked the inner door. As he closed both doors, she trudged up a flight of stairs to the first floor. She unlocked the door, walked inside, and waited for him to follow.

He stepped into her living room and color surrounded him. Her couch was a dusky red, with blue, yellow and green throw pillows. Three paintings hung on the walls – two of beaches, one of a mountain meadow covered with wildflowers.

The varnish on her hardwood floors was yellowed with age. An Oriental rug covered the center, its vibrant blues, reds and greens shimmering in the soft light.

Crammed-full bookcases lined the walls, and a stack of magazines rose haphazardly on an end table next to the couch.

"Nice place," he said. "Why did you move out of the high rise?"

She unzipped her running jacket and hung it on the coat tree at the door. The tight shirt she wore outlined her running bra. It made him want to trace the contours of her body. Peel the bra off of her. Find what it was hiding.

"This was Cilla's place. She wanted to move in with

Brendan, but she had six months left on her lease. My lease was up, so I moved here. I have a lot more room for about the same amount of money."

"Have a seat," she said, hovering in a doorway that led to the dining room. "I'm going to make some tea. You want some?"

"No, thanks." He shifted his feet, glancing at the couch. He wasn't going to sit down while she was standing. "I'm a coffee person."

"You want a cup?"

"Thanks, but don't bother. Too much work for one cup."

"No work at all." She flashed him a smile, and one side of his mouth turned up in response. "My brother gave me one of those fancy single cup coffeemakers last year for Christmas. I don't use it much, but you're welcome to a cup."

"Okay, then. That would be great."

"Come into the kitchen, then, and pick out your fancy flavor."

She disappeared into the kitchen, and as he followed her, he thought about how much things had changed. Three days ago, Livvy Marini inviting him into her home was unimaginable. Now he was standing in her living room, being offered coffee.

Her kitchen was cramped, with barely enough room for a tiny table. But it was neat and tidy. No dishes in the sink.

"The pods are in the pantry," she said, opening a door next to the sink. "Help yourself."

The pantry was a tiny closet, lined with shelves holding glasses and dishes, boxes of pasta and jars of flour and sugar, cans of tomatoes. A metal rack holding the small coffee pods stood in the corner. He grabbed the first one he saw and backed out of the space.

Livvy stood at the sink, filling a kettle, and he squeezed past her to the coffee machine. There was less space than he'd realized, because he brushed her butt with his hip.

She froze.

"Sorry," he muttered. "Thought there was more room."

"Don't worry about it," she said, a little breathless. "It's a tight fit in here."

A tight fit.

He turned his back, trying to block out the images flooding his brain. When she finished with the kettle, he filled the coffee maker. Started the coffee brewing and slid past her, pressing against the table to avoid touching her again.

He didn't exhale until he was in the living room.

He stared out the window, pretending he was fascinated by the street below her building. *Get hold of yourself. You're not getting involved with her.*

A few minutes later, she emerged from the kitchen holding his coffee. Setting it down on the coffee table, she said, "Sit down, Ward. The couch isn't booby trapped. I'll be right out."

She disappeared toward the kitchen, and moments later he heard water running. She was in the bathroom. Finally she emerged, her face red and shiny. She'd cleaned off the traces of tears on her face.

After fetching her tea from the kitchen, she turned on two lamps that cast a golden glow over the room, then sat on the couch. He lowered himself onto the other end. Watching him over the rim of her mug, she said, "So why were you chasing me tonight?"

Ryan took another sip of his coffee, sighed and set it on the table. "I'd been on that path for an hour already. Watching for you."

"*Watching* for me?" She frowned. "Were you just standing there, looking at everyone as they ran by?"

He shrugged. "Nope. I was running. I had your old address at the New York Building, so I figured that underpass in front of it was where you'd get on the path. I ran up and down, staying close to the ramp. When you showed up, I ran after you."

He set the coffee carefully on the table. "I wasn't trying to frighten you. It was damn cold on that path, so I put up the hood on my sweatshirt. It didn't occur to me that you wouldn't be able to see my face."

He'd thought she'd recognize him immediately. Stupid of him. Almost as stupid as chasing her down the way he had.

"Okay." She'd curled her fingers around her mug, as if she were still cold. "I still don't understand why you were watching for me, though."

"After I left you at the station, a black car followed me. Toyota Corolla. Matte paint on the hood."

Her hand shook violently as she set the mug on the table. A tiny splash of tea spilled out, and she hurried into the kitchen. Came back with a paper towel and wiped it up, her hand trembling.

"Yeah," he said grimly. "Has to be the same one you saw. It hung around most of the day. I couldn't see the guy's face, because I'm on the third floor. But he was there for several hours. When I came out to head over to the lake, it was gone."

She paled a little, clutching the tea to her chest. It rose and fell with an unsteady breath. "I knew I should have taken Cilla when I talked to Freddie Sampson. She would have known what kind of car it was." Her mouth trembled a little. "She would have been able to tell you the make, model and probably the year. Maybe we could have tracked it down."

He raised one eyebrow. "Your sister is a gearhead?"

"Yeah." The trembling turned into a shaky smile. "My father owned car repair places. Cilla hung out with him at one of them, working on Betsy."

"Betsy?"

"Her car. It's an old Mustang."

"You didn't soak up any of her knowledge, though."

"Nope. I wasn't interested in cars."

He couldn't stop himself from leaning a little closer.

"What were you interested in?"

"Books. Movies." Her mouth curled into a tiny smile. "Boys."

"Is that right?" He edged closer. "And did you spend a lot of time with *your* interests?"

She took another sip of her tea. The muscles in her neck worked as she swallowed, and her shoulders dropped. Her tiny smile wasn't trembling as much. "I saw a bunch of movies," she offered. "Read a lot of books."

"And the boys? Did you catch a lot of them?" He held his breath, wondering what she would say.

"Sadly, no." She tucked an errant strand of hair behind her ear, and he wanted to lean forward and do it for her. Let the silky strands flow through his fingers. "I was too shy to actually talk to any of them. So I yearned at a distance."

His heart thumped hard against his chest and other parts of him were pounding as well. "You still too shy to talk to the boys?"

"I'm talking to you, aren't I?" Her eyes locked with his, her pupils dilated. The green of her iris was a barely-there rim around the black.

She was as turned on as he was.

She held his gaze for a few seconds too long. Then she stood up abruptly. Nervous?

"I'm hungry. There's a good pizza place close by. They deliver."

"I don't want to misunderstand," he said, swallowing hard. "Are you asking me to stay?" he asked. He was hungry, too. Starving, in fact. But food was the least of it.

Holding his gaze, she nodded slowly. "I'm asking."

CHAPTER SEVEN

"Good," Livvy said, her heart banging against her ribs like she'd run ten miles. "I'll order a pizza. What do you like?"

"I'm good with anything except anchovies. Or eggs." Ryan wrinkled his nose. "Why would you ruin a perfectly good pizza with an egg?"

"You don't like your pizza all gooey and slippery?" she teased.

Ryan's pupils grew wider, until no color remained. The planes of his face sharpened.

Oh. Heat blasted through her, warming everything. Especially...Oh, my God.

"I'm a big fan of slippery and gooey." His voice was a low rumble of sex and lust. "Not for *dinner*, though."

Her legs grew rubbery, and she backed against the door as she picked up her phone. Her hand trembled, and she gripped the phone more tightly. "Okay," she whispered. "No egg."

She stared at the phone, mind empty of everything except the pictures his words had evoked. Graphic, X-rated pictures.

"You gonna call?" he asked. "You want me to do it?"

She lifted her head. He was staring at her, focused and intent. Waiting for her to move, so he could pounce. She swallowed hard, unable to look away. Cornered.

He'd already hunted her once tonight. And when he'd caught her, he'd been gentle. Sweet. Caring.

In the past, thinking of herself as prey and a man as the hunter implied vulnerability. Helplessness. That would have offended her feminist self. Pissed her off. Tonight? The thought made her knees weak.

When he rose from the couch, she forced herself to look back at her phone. Scroll through her contacts until she saw the pizza place a few blocks away. Stabbing the 'call' icon, she swallowed again.

"Genoa Pizza," a perky female voice said. "Can I help you?"

"A pizza," she managed to say. "For delivery. Pepperoni and mushrooms."

Two minutes later, she'd given the woman her phone number and address. She had no idea what kind of pizza she'd ordered. "Thirty-five minutes," the woman said.

"Thank you." Livvy ended the call and dropped her phone on the table by the door. "We have thirty-five minutes," she said. "To wait," she added too quickly, her tongue tripping over the words. "Until the pizza gets here."

"I'm sure we can think of a way to amuse ourselves," he said, holding her gaze as he lowered himself back onto the couch. Not as far in the corner now.

She was certain they could. Watching Ryan watch her, his face taut, a slash of red on both cheekbones, she was afraid his ideas were identical to hers.

Returning to the couch, she dropped onto the cushion in the corner. As far away from him as she could get.

Not far enough, her prim, rational mind retorted.

She didn't want to be prim tonight.

Instead of moving closer, as she'd expected him to do, he frowned. Sat up straighter. "You're limping."

"I am?" She glanced down at her feet, as if expecting a flashing red light on one shoe.

"Your left foot. Did you hurt it while you were running?"

"I don't remember." She frowned, tentatively scrunching her foot in the running shoe. "It hurts, though."

He slid across the couch until he was close enough to grasp her foot. His fingers curled around her ankle, his hand warm even through her running tights. "May I take a look?"

"Uh." Heat from his hand crawled up her leg, heading straight to a danger zone. She should move her foot. Back away from Ryan. But all she could manage with her short-circuited brain was an uh? She cleared her throat. "Okay."

She bent to unlace her running shoe, but he gently pushed her hand aside. "Let me."

He lifted her foot onto his thigh and tugged at one end of the lace. It fell open, and he wiggled a finger beneath the laces on the top of her foot to loosen them. Finally, cupping her calf in the palm of his hand, he worked the shoe off her foot.

Suddenly self-conscious, Livvy curled her toes in the short running sock. "I'm good," she said, reaching for her foot.

"No, you're not," he said, sliding his palm over the bottom of her foot, caressing her from toes to heel. "You're hurt."

The touch of his hand made her squirm. And not because she was ticklish.

"Ticklish?" he said, glancing up at her with a tiny grin. As if he knew why she was squirming.

"Yeah," she said, swallowing. "Guess so."

He peeled the sock away and dropped it on the floor. "You don't know?" He raised one eyebrow as he trailed a finger down her foot again. The rasp of his finger against her bare skin made her suck in a breath. Shift on the couch, restless. Needy.

"Yes. I mean no." Irritated at the way her brain was

leaking out of her ears, she swallowed hard. "It's fine now."

Ignoring her, he bent her foot back and peered at the sole of her foot. "You have a bruise here." He skimmed the middle of her arch, his finger barely touching. Her eyes fluttered closed. Sparks shot out of the bottom of her foot, and not because it was bruised. "Looks like you stepped on something."

"Wow." She swallowed again, forced her eyes open and tried to tug her foot away. Time to find some game. "Hope it won't have to be amputated."

"I think your pain can be relieved without resorting to drastic measures." He pressed his thumb into the muscle and massaged it, and her eyes tried to roll back in her head. Holding her gaze, his eyes dark and knowing, he murmured, "I'm sure we can come up with more...specialized care."

"What...what did you have in mind?" she managed to ask.

"I think we'll have to do some testing." His hand closed around her foot, letting his fingers trail fire over her arch. "Find out what feels the best."

You, she almost blurted as her eyes closed. *You feel the best.*

He shifted on the couch, and her eyes fluttered open. Her heel rested on his thigh. If she bent her foot forward, she could touch the bulge in his jeans.

Not that she wanted her foot on that bulge.

Yes, she did. Mostly, she wanted her hands there. Her mouth. Other parts of her body.

"Ryan," she whispered, drawing her foot away from him. "What are we doing?"

He edged closer to her. Close enough that she could feel the heat pouring off his body. His hand was inches from hers. "If you don't know, I must be doing something wrong. Do you want me to explain?"

Yes. Please. In detail. "Give me a hint," she said. She leaned toward him as if she was a magnet and he was iron.

Her gaze dropped to the front of his jeans again. *Don't*

think about iron.

"We're talking about your treatment," he said, his low voice making every nerve in her body prickle. "It involves long, slow… consultations. Deep concentrations of…heat. Lots of hand to body… manipulations."

Heat swept over her body, scorching every inch of her. She wanted to pull him closer. Rip off his clothes. Explore some of those slow consultations. Those hand to body manipulations.

She slid her hands beneath her thighs to keep from reaching for him. "Not sure I can handle that much…treatment."

"Oh, I think you're up to it, Livvy." His voice was ragged. Not quite steady. He edged closer. "If you need some help getting ready, I'd be happy to help you out."

"That's a generous offer," she managed to say. "But I wouldn't want to take advantage of you."

"Take advantage," he said, sliding close enough for her to feel his breath on her neck. "Please."

"Maybe we need one of those long, slow consultations," she whispered.

His gaze dropped to her mouth, and he brushed the pad of his finger over her lips. "Let's find out," he murmured.

His eyes fluttered closed as his nose bumped hers. He barely touched her lips, sliding his mouth along hers. Tasting, touching with the tip of his tongue, until he gently sucked her lower lip into his mouth.

Someone moaned. It might have been her. Then he wrapped his arms around her and pulled her onto his lap. His body surrounded her, holding her tight against him. Cutting off all avenues of escape. He traced her cheekbones, smoothed over her ear, finally touched her mouth. The pads of his fingers teased her, barely touching.

Her mouth fell open, and his lips found hers immediately.

Their mouths fused together. When he slid his tongue along the sensitive skin inside her lips, she opened to him.

Let her tongue tangle with his. Explored his mouth, drinking in the tiny sounds he made.

She wanted to remember everything. The way his hands clutched at her, holding her as if he was afraid she'd disappear. The rich taste of the coffee she'd made for him. The hardness of his body against hers.

She wanted more than that. She needed to touch his skin. Taste him. Feel his muscles twitch as she trailed her mouth over him. Drink in his scent.

She wanted to see his chest, hidden beneath that hoodie. She yearned to press her palms against his muscles. Did he have hair there? Would it be soft against her fingers?

He groaned into her mouth and speared his hands into her hair. Held her head steady as he plundered.

She moved against him, unable to stop herself. He'd barely touched her, and she was so tightly wound she was ready to explode. She shifted in his lap so she faced him and pressed closer. Moaned when the hard length in his jeans pressed exactly where she needed it.

She shoved her hands beneath his tee shirt, letting her fingers dance over his rock-hard abs. They twitched against her palms, and he lifted his mouth from hers to suck at the tendon in her neck. He held her hips tight, pressing her hard against him.

"Touch me," she whispered, turning her head to find his mouth again. "I want your hands on me."

"God, Livvy." He lifted his head and stared at her. His mouth was wet, his eyes hugely dilated. His hands shook as he brushed her hair away from her face. Then he smoothed his palms down her body to the hem of her running shirt. "You sure?"

"Yes. Please." His muscles jumped beneath her fingers as she slid her hands up to his chest. He jerked against her when she found the hard nubs of his nipples. Sucked in a breath when she shoved his shirt up and licked one, then the other.

"You're a fast learner," he breathed into her ear, gently

nipping the sensitive lobe. "You've got this treatment thing down." She gasped when he lifted her shirt and trailed his callused fingers over her belly.

He traced each of her ribs as he moved upward, until she was writhing against him, her tongue dancing with his. When he reached her running bra, he tried to slip his hand beneath the thick elastic that held it in place. But it was too tight. He could only get one finger beneath the elastic.

"Jesus, Marini. Is this some kind of chastity bra?" He pulled out his finger, let the band snap back into place and danced his fingers over the slick material instead. He cupped her breasts, testing the weight of them in his hands. Crept close to her nipples, but never touched them.

She ground her mouth into his, tangled their tongues. "Take it off," she panted. "Now. Get rid of it."

Ryan lifted her tee shirt. He'd begun to draw it over her head when the buzzer rang. Stopped. Rang again.

Her eyes flew open and she stared at him. His eyes were completely dark, his face taut with arousal. "The pizza," she whispered.

"Not interested in pizza," he murmured, tugging at her lobe.

The doorbell rang again, and he slid his thumbs over her nipples. She bit her lip to keep from crying out. Pressed into his hands for a long moment.

Then she closed her eyes and took a deep breath. Tried to steady herself. Couldn't quite manage.

Tugging her shirt down with a trembling hand, she clambered off his lap, stumbling when she tried to stand up. Ryan stood, as well, shifting from side to side as if to relieve the pressure at his groin. "I'll get it," he said, reaching for his wallet.

"You can't go to the door like that," she said, running her hand lightly over the hard ridge of his penis, hidden beneath the denim.

"God, Livvy," he groaned. "Not helping."

"I'll get it," she said, pressing the button to unlock the

door downstairs. She shoved her hands through her hopelessly tangled hair, afraid the delivery guy would know exactly what they'd been doing.

Fumbling in her bag as she heard the guy climbing the stairs, she found her wallet and extracted some bills with shaking hands. It was far too much, but maybe he'd be so awed by his tip that he wouldn't notice the sex vibes swirling through her living room.

When he knocked on the door, she opened it and shoved the money at him. "Thanks, Teddy," she said, grabbing the box from his hands. "See you next time."

"You got it, Livvy," the kid said, widening his eyes at the amount of money she'd given him. "Wow! Thanks, Liv."

"You're welcome," she said as she closed the door.

Leaning against it, she watched the pizza box wobble in her shaky hands. Damn it! Had Teddy and the pizza been an unwelcome interruption?

Or had he rung her doorbell in the nick of time?

Unwelcome. And just in the nick of time.

Swallowing hard, she tottered over to the couch and dropped the box on the coffee table. "You want a beer? A glass of wine?"

"Neither," he said, his eyes locked on hers. "Pizza can wait. It'll reheat."

She dropped onto the arm of the couch. "Yeah. It will." She stared at her visibly trembling hands. Arousal swirled through her, sharp and insistent. "But maybe we need to think about this a little more."

"I've been thinking about it since the moment I saw you at the conservatory." He wrapped an arm around her waist and bounced her onto the cushion beside him. Tucked her against him. "Believe me, I've studied it from every angle. Don't see a downside here."

He caressed her upper arm as if it was normal for them to be sitting so close together. As if they made out on her couch all the time.

She didn't move away. "Teddy ringing my bell was kind

of a mood killer," she finally said.

"I thought *I* was ringing your bell." His fingertips shivered over her ear, and she sucked in a breath. Quivered.

"You were," she said, sitting up reluctantly. This was a mistake. They were working together. She couldn't get involved with him. "Until Teddy showed up and I came to my senses."

You want him. You know you do. Who would find out? The devil sat on her shoulder, whispering temptation into her ear. Her breath sawed in and out.

"This wasn't a good idea," she finally said.

"Really? I think it was one of the all-time great ideas." He took her hand and angled to face her. "Why don't you think so?"

She swallowed. Stood up. "We're working together, Ryan. What if Bates' defense attorney found out we were sleeping together? He might try to get all the evidence we collect thrown out of court."

"You think we're going to be talking about Bates' case in bed?" He stood, as well. "Believe me, Livvy, I won't be thinking about anything but you. And I'll make sure you're not thinking of anything else when we're..."

She slapped her palm over his mouth. "God. Don't say it. It's hard enough when you're not talking about it."

He pressed a kiss to her palm. "You're gonna be the responsible adult?"

"Someone has to be," she muttered as she let her hand drop away from his mouth. Breathed in. Out. "Beer or wine?"

He held her gaze for a long moment. Longing swirled through his eyes. His whole body canted toward her, as if an invisible cord already bound them together. "Beer's good," he finally said.

She fled to the kitchen, where she opened two bottles of Blue Moon and carried them back to the living room, along with plates and napkins. The bottles clinked together in her right hand as she walked, the rhythmic noise beating out a tattoo of *do it. Do it. Do it.*

She sat next to him on the couch, their thighs touching. Neither of them said much while they ate. Heat leached through his jeans and her running tights, making her ache for more. She wanted to feel his skin against hers. She wanted to tangle her foot around his. Press her calf against his.

She wanted to say 'the hell with the job'.

Instead, she took another bite of pizza. She didn't taste it. All she could taste was Ryan's mouth on hers.

After Ryan ate the last piece of pizza, he stood up. "I'm going to go. Give you a chance to think without being distracted."

"You think you're a distraction, Ward?" she tossed back before she thought.

"Possibly." A tiny grin played at the corners of his mouth. "You tell me, Livvy." He leaned closer, until she could see the golden flecks glittering in his eyes. "I don't want to pressure you. I want you to come to me because you can't stay away. I want you to want me as much as I want you."

I already do, she wanted to say.

Instead, she said, "Thank you." She tugged at the front of his sweatshirt to bring him closer. "See you tomorrow."

"You will." He backed her toward the door, pressed her hard against it. "Just in case you've forgotten…" He took her mouth, sweeping his tongue along hers, tangling them together. He tasted of beer and pizza and Ryan.

She was melting into him when he broke away. "I'll see you tomorrow. Don't forget about," he touched her lips, "this."

He slipped out the door, waited on the landing until he heard her lock engage. As she listened to his footsteps getting fainter, she slid to the floor, her fingers touching her mouth.

"I won't forget."

CHAPTER EIGHT

It was still dark when Livvy woke to the insistent buzzing of her phone. Fumbling on her night table, she finally closed her fingers around it and flopped onto her back. Stabbed the 'call' button.

"This better be good," she said, her voice sharp with irritation.

"Good morning to you, too, Liv. This is Brendan. Your future brother-in-law."

"Hey, Bren," Livvy said, struggling to sit up. "Sorry. I thought it was someone from work."

"No worries. I'm used to cranky in the morning. Your sister is even worse than you."

"You, on the other hand, sound disgustingly chipper for this ungodly hour." Livvy glanced at the clock. Six-thirty a.m.

"You'd sound chipper too, if you woke up to a gorgeous woman kiss…"

"You're talking to my sister, you jerk." Cilla's voice in the background. "Watch what you're saying, or you won't be waking up like that again anytime soon."

"Right. Anyway, Liv, the reason I'm calling so early is that I have to be in court all afternoon. My testimony got bumped forward. So I'm going to round up Philby as soon as I'm showered and dressed. Want to meet me at the station in about an hour?"

"Sounds great, Brendan. Thanks."

"See you later," he said and hung up.

She was heading out the door forty-five minutes later when her phone rang again. Brendan. Pressing the call button, she said, "I was just walking out the door. Fifteen minutes, tops."

"You don't have to hurry," Brendan said. The murmur of several different voices hummed in the background. "Philby's dead. Best time of death estimate is four hours ago."

Livvy dropped her bag onto the floor and stumbled into a chair. "From the number of people I hear in the background, I'm guessing it wasn't a suicide. Or an accident."

"No," Brendan said, his voice grim. "It was an execution. I found him on the floor near the front door. My theory? Someone woke him up, Philby opened the door, the guy stepped inside and put the gun to his head. Two shots. Between the eyes."

Nausea roiled Livvy's stomach. *She'd* sent Brendan there. *She* was the one who'd gone to Freddie Sampson's house. Orchestrated Jerry Williams visit to Connor's station.

Was she responsible for Philby's death? Yes. She was.

"Oh, my God," she said, her voice muted with shock. "What should I...what do you do now?"

"The first thing I want you to do is go to my station. Stay there. I don't know how long I'll be at the scene, but I want to make sure you're safe. You understand?"

She'd never heard Brendan's cop voice. The one that issued orders instead of asking. She swallowed. "Yes. I'll go straight to your station."

"Don't stop for coffee or breakfast," he ordered. "In fact, I'll send a squad car to follow you in."

"Don't do that," she said. "I'll get there safely. I'll be really careful."

"You want Cilla to come over?"

"No. My car's in the garage. I can walk down the rear stairs and get right in. I'll be fine. Go do your job, Bren. And thanks for the heads-up." She ended the call before Brendan could reply.

Her hand shook as she picked up her briefcase and headed toward the rear of her house. *Ryan.* She stumbled to a stop. He needed to know. He'd given her Philby's name.

She sank into a chair at her tiny kitchen table and pulled up his contact info. Touched the call button.

"Ward," he said, his voice rough with sleep.

"Ryan, it's Livvy," she said.

"Hey." She heard his bedding rustle, as if he sat up. "Good morning. How are you doing?" His voice got even rougher. "Did you miss me last night?"

"Yes," she said softly. "I did." She wasn't going to lie to him. "But that's not why I called." She swallowed. "I just got off the phone with Brendan. He went to Carl Philby's house and found him dead. Shot twice in the head."

Silence. Then, "What did he tell you to do?" All the softness in Ryan's voice had disappeared. Now he sounded just like Brendan. Hard. Taking control.

"He told me to go to his station. I was walking out the door when he called."

"Are you on your way there?" Ryan asked sharply.

"No. I'm still at home. I called you first." She took a shaky breath. "Since you gave me Philby's name."

"Thank God. Stay where you are. I'm on my way over. Be there in fifteen."

"You don't have to…"

"Don't leave your place, Livvy," he interrupted. "I'll be right there."

78

"Okay. I'll wait for you."

"Good." The phone went dead. Livvy slid it into the pocket of her briefcase and headed back to the living room. She wandered to the windows and looked through the bare tree branches at the street below her. There was nothing out of the ordinary. A few people hurried down the sidewalk, heading toward a bus stop or an El station. The street was a patchwork of empty parking spots along the curb. It looked like any other morning.

Except a man was dead. A man she'd put in the crosshairs.

And from the way Brendan and Ryan had acted, she might need to watch her back, as well.

Twenty minutes later, her buzzer rang insistently. She peered out the window and saw Ryan standing in front of the door. He wore the same hoody he'd had on last night and his hair looked as if someone had taken an eggbeater to it.

She pushed the lock release in her apartment and waited until he knocked on the door. Looked through her peep hole to make sure it was him.

When she opened the door, he stepped inside and wrapped his arms around her. Buried his face in her hair. "You okay?" he murmured against her head.

"Shaken up. Horribly guilty." Winding her arms around his waist, she crowded close to the comforting breadth of his chest. "But otherwise okay."

"Not your fault," he said immediately. His arms tightened around her. "Bates' fault."

His voice was as cold as the winter wind that gusted off Lake Michigan. She clutched him for a long moment, then leaned away. "You and Brendan both scared the crap out of me. 'Stay in your apartment.' 'I'll send a squad car.' 'Don't move.'"

"Thank God Donovan didn't have his head up his ass." He cupped her cheek and leaned forward to brush a kiss over her lips. "And thank God you were smart enough to call me."

"You didn't mind?" she asked. "I know I woke you up."

"Not only do I not mind, I would have been pissed off if you hadn't. I'm the one who told you to contact Philby." He closed his eyes and pressed his forehead to hers. "I'm driving you into Donovan's station, and I'm staying."

"You don't have to do that," she said, leaning back to study his face. She couldn't help running her fingers through the soft waves of his hair, trying to tame it. "You ran out of your place without even combing your hair."

"Who's gonna give a damn about my hair?" But he smoothed a hand over his head. "You ready to go?"

"Just need my briefcase." She spotted it sitting on the radiator cover in front of the window and grabbed it. "All set."

He clamped his fingers around her wrist. "You were standing at the window?"

"Yes," she said, easing her hand away from the handcuff of his and pressing their palms together instead. "Brendan freaked me out, and you doubled down on it. I was looking for anything that looked out of place. Different."

"Everything looked the same as always. Right?"

When she nodded, he laced their fingers together. "If someone is waiting for you out there, you're not going to see him. Keep your blinds closed and stay away from the windows. I'll put a better lock on your back door today."

She frowned at him. "There's nothing wrong with my lock."

"It's a piece of shit lock. Anyone who wanted to get in here would have it open in about thirty seconds."

"How do you even know what kind of lock I have?" She glanced at her back door, seeing a lock that looked like a million others.

"I can see that pitiful thing from here." He curled his arm around her shoulders, squeezed once, then let her go. "Let's go. Stay behind me."

He trotted down the stairs, and Livvy followed, her heart

racing. She'd been nervous before, but now she was terrified. Was it really possible that someone was watching for her? Parked on her street, waiting for her to leave?

Before Ryan opened the front door, he shoved the side of his hoodie back and put his hand on his gun. The weapon was large. Matte black. Ominous-looking.

Finally he stepped outside, his hand still on his weapon. He scanned the street for a long moment, then nodded at her to step out.

He hustled her toward a black SUV, opened the door and practically shoved her inside. Then he ran around to the driver's side, slid in and turned the car on. In a handful of seconds, her building was two blocks behind them.

"Got you a coffee," he said, nodding at the cup holders beneath the console.

"Thank you," she said, reaching for it. "If I wasn't belted in, I'd kiss you."

"I'll take a rain check," he said, his expression relaxing for the first time since she'd opened her door to him.

She took a gulp of the still-hot coffee, then drew in a deep breath. "You didn't have to do this, you know. Come over before you'd even showered. Take me into Brendan's station."

"I know." He glanced over at her. "I wanted to do it. This Bates mess just got a lot messier. A lot more dangerous. And it's my fault you're sucked into it."

"That's not true," she said, swiveling to face him. "If I wasn't working with you, I'd still be working on the Bates case. I'd just be working with someone else."

"I'm the one who gave you those names," he said, his voice grim. "I could have talked to them myself."

"You said they wouldn't talk to you," she said immediately, pleased she'd remembered that detail. "So that was never an option."

"Smart ass," he muttered under his breath as he turned into the parking lot at Brendan's station. "Let's go inside and see what Donovan has."

* * *

Thirty minutes later, clutching a bakery bag and holding a tray of coffees, Ryan pushed through the doors of the nineteenth district. He'd dropped Livvy off, escorted her to the conference room, made sure the desk sergeant knew where she was, then ducked out again.

As he climbed the stairs, he heard the rumble of voices from the conference room above him. A man's voice. Then Livvy's.

"Ryan drove me here." Silence, as if Livvy was composing herself. "He told me Philby would fold if we pressed him." Ryan heard the wobble in her voice. "It's my fault he's dead."

"Ryan?" It sounded like Brendan Donovan. Ward reached the top of the stairs and hesitated at the door.

"Ryan Ward. The guy I'm working with on the Bates case. You know who he is."

"Damn right I know who Ryan fucking Ward is. Why did he drive you over here?"

"Because he wanted to make sure I was safe." A chair scraped against the floor. "What's your problem, Brendan?"

"You're part of my family now. We take care of our own."

"I can take care of myself. And if I need help, I'll call whoever I want."

"Did you forget what that asshole did to Cilla?"

"I haven't forgotten a thing, Brendan," Livvy said sharply. "But my sister's forgiven him and moved on. You should do the same."

Ryan's hand tightened on the coffee holder. Livvy was defending him to Brendan Donovan. Her future brother-in-law. The guy Ryan had confronted at the hospital after Jack Murphy'd been shot.

Warmth slid through him. Livvy was taking his side. Telling Donovan to back down. His throat thickened and he struggled to swallow the lump.

Shame and guilt spilled through him whenever he thought about what he'd done to Cilla Marini. Livvy's sister. This was his opportunity to make some amends. He'd watch out for Cilla's sister. Make sure Livvy didn't get hurt. Make sure Bates couldn't ruin another life.

"Forgiveness isn't that easy, Liv," Donovan said.

"It's exactly that easy," Livvy retorted.

Ryan was close enough to the door to see Livvy nose to nose with Brendan. She held Donovan's gaze for a long, tense moment. Finally Brendan raised his hands and stepped back.

Ryan had heard enough. Time for Brendan to stop haranguing Livvy. He strolled into the room, set the coffee on the table. Lifted one out and handed it to Livvy, passed her the bag with bagels and cream cheese. Then he turned to Brendan. "Donovan. You need coffee? A bagel?"

Brendan stared at him with cold eyes. "Don't need anything from you, Ward."

Ryan shrugged one shoulder. "Suit yourself." He chose a bagel for himself, lifted another of the coffees out of the holder, and sat down at the conference table. Across from Livvy. No way was he going to fan the flames of Donovan's temper by cozying up to Livvy.

To his surprise, she pushed her bagel across the table, then walked around to sit next to him. Clearly choosing sides.

Livvy lifted her chin at Brendan, as if daring him to challenge her. Donovan narrowed his eyes at her. "*Him? Really, Liv?*"

"None of your damn business, Brendan Donovan."

"You gonna bring him to dinner?" Brendan crossed his arms over his chest.

"Maybe," she said, examining the bagels before pulling one out.

"There'll be a lot of chest-thumping if you do." Donovan scowled at her.

"You know I like a good show," she said, opening the cream cheese.

Donovan stared at her. She held his gaze a heartbeat too long, then calmly spread cream cheese on her bagel before passing the tub to Ryan.

"You enjoying this, Ward?" Brendan finally said. "Is that why you're sticking around?"

"I always appreciate a good melodrama," Ryan said. "But I'm here because *I* sent her to Philby. Figured you'd need my input."

Donovan scowled at him, but didn't say a thing. Ryan's lips twitched, but he didn't let the smirk out. Livvy had beaten Donovan at his game. On top of that, Ryan was right and Donovan knew it. They needed to pool their information if they hoped to catch Philby's murderer.

The room was silent, tension bouncing off the gray walls, as Ryan chewed a poppyseed bagel and watched Livvy eat hers. He'd been stupidly delighted when she'd chosen poppyseed, too. Were they going to be one of those couples? The ones who seemed to have a mind-meld?

His hand shook a little as he lifted his coffee. *No.* They weren't going to be a couple at all. He needed to straighten out his life before he could get involved in a relationship. He and Livvy could have fun, but it would end when this case ended. She deserved better than him.

And *he* needed to get his act together before he tried to be part of a couple.

Livvy brushed the bagel crumbs off her hands, took another sip of coffee, and turned to Brendan. "All right, Brendan, what did you find at Philby's place?"

Donovan's gaze snapped over to Ryan, then back to Livvy. "Pretty much what I told you. Nothing else in his place was disturbed. No footprints. No casings left behind. We have the techs dusting for fingerprints, but I'm guessing nothing will pop."

"Sounds professional," Ryan said.

Donovan glanced at him and nodded reluctantly. As if

he hated to agree with anything Ryan said. "Looks like it."

Ryan turned to Livvy. Her foot bounced against the floor, and her fingers drummed on the tabletop. He wanted to reach over and put his hand over hers. Help her settle. But not with Donovan in the room.

He didn't care if Donovan got into it with him. But he didn't want the guy going after Livvy when he wasn't around.

Before Donovan could continue, Cilla Marini walked in, followed by a short woman with tousled blond hair. Katya Sobieski. She used to work in Ryan's district. "Hey, Bren," Cilla said.

Donovan turned and held her for a moment, then hugged the blond woman. "Thanks for coming over, Cil. You, too, Katya."

Cilla spotted her sister sitting beside Ryan and hurried over. Livvy stood up, and Cilla hugged her tightly. "How are you doing?" Cilla murmured.

"Better." Livvy glanced at Ryan, and the tension around her eyes eased. A tiny smile lifted one corner of her mouth.

Cilla switched her gaze to Ryan. "Ward. What are you doing here?" There was no animosity in her voice. No hostility. Just curiosity.

"I'm working with Livvy on the Bates case," he said. "I'm the one who gave her Philby's name."

"Oh." Cilla raised her eyebrows, her gaze snapping from him to Livvy and back again. "Interesting."

"Gus Swenson playing his usual games," Livvy said.

Cilla nodded to the blond, who was talking to Donovan. "You know Katya, don't you, Ward?"

"Yeah, we used to work together." He nodded at the blond. "She transferred out after that mess with her partner, Henry Bennett and that serial rapist you caught."

"She's in the sixteenth now. Passed the detective's exam last month." Cilla grinned at Sobieski. "Since Bren and I can't be partners, I settled for Katya," she said.

Sobieski raised one eyebrow. "You lucked out and you

know it, Marini."

Before Cilla could answer, Connor, Quinn and Mia crowded into the room. In seconds, all the Donovans, as well as Cilla and Sobieski, were talking at once. Livvy joined in, clearly at home with the Donovan family. Ryan watched the give and take, the easy flow of conversation in the close-knit group, and he swallowed. The Donovans were nothing like his family.

A sharp stab of loneliness speared through him, even in the midst of so many people. He was the outsider here. The stranger. Tolerated only because he had information they needed.

Even Sobieski was part of the group.

A hand settled on his back. Ryan glanced up and saw Livvy standing beside him. She was talking to her sister, but she squeezed his shoulder gently.

Including him.

Letting him know she hadn't forgotten him.

He wanted to reach for her, to thank her. Instead, he pressed his fingers into the table, hard enough to whiten his knuckles.

He wouldn't do that to her. Not in front of the Donovan family.

Before he could give into temptation, Brendan whistled. The sharp, piercing sound made everyone freeze.

"We need to exchange some info. Katya, you used to work the twenty-second, where Philby was killed. Cilla, you, Livvy and," he hesitated for a fraction of a second, "Ward are familiar with the Bates investigation. You three jokers," he nodded at Connor, Quinn and Mia, "are pretty much worthless on this case, so you can get lost. Let's get down to business."

In moments, the other Donovan siblings had vanished and everyone else sat around the table. Livvy reclaimed her seat next to him. As Brendan began talking again, Livvy wrapped her foot around his. Nudged her knee against his, and left it there.

Ryan swallowed the giant lump in his throat. She was lining up on his side. Drawing him into the Donovan circle.

He didn't know about the Donovans. Wasn't sure they could ever accept him as part of their circle. Wasn't sure he'd even *want* to be part of the Donovan circle. But he sure as hell wanted Livvy on his side. As close as she could possibly get.

CHAPTER NINE

An hour later, Livvy's shoulders relaxed as she walked out of the nineteenth district station beside Ryan. After the initial chest thumping, Brendan had calmed down and treated Ryan like a colleague. A fellow cop who could help with his investigation.

There were moments of snark, but for the most part, everyone had behaved. Cooperated like actual adults. They had a plan.

"Thank you for reminding Brendan to start sweating Jerry Williams and Freddie Sampson," she said as she slid into his car.

Ryan shrugged as he tugged on his seat belt. "He's a good cop. He would have done it anyway. I know those meatheads, though. Williams will be easier to crack than Sampson, which is why I suggested Donovan start with Jerry. But both of those losers need to know the deal."

"Yeah," Livvy said. She glanced at Ryan, wondering if he realized he'd called Brendan a good cop. "Once they know what happened to Philby, even those two jokers will realize they might be next in line for a late-night visit.

Offering them protective custody in exchange for testimony might loosen their tongues." She rolled her shoulders, feeling the tension ease. "I planned to talk to Gus today, anyway. I'll tell him we'll need to work something out with Sampson and Williams if they're willing to testify against Bates."

Ryan glanced at her as he stopped at a red light. "I'll drop you off at the Daley Center."

"You don't have to do that." She scanned a work email, then slid her phone back into her briefcase. "You said you were going back to your apartment. My office is in the opposite direction. Drop me at my place and I'll drive in myself."

A muscle in Ryan's jaw jumped. "Not happening. Bates is in clean-up mode. I don't want you wandering around by yourself." He swiveled to look at her. "Where do you park when you drive to the Daley Center building?"

"The office rents a floor at one of the parking garages."

His hands tightened on the steering wheel and the car leaped ahead when the light turned green. "You really want to walk through a dark parking garage by yourself? With every car a possible hiding place? I thought you were smarter than that, Livvy."

Ryan's words sent a chill shivering down her spine. They were a reminder she was involved in a nasty case. With a lot at stake. "You're right. I hadn't thought about that creepy parking garage." She spotted El tracks a few block away. "Drop me off at that Red Line station. I'll take the El."

"Now you're just jerking me around." He accelerated through a yellow light, accompanied by the flash from the red light camera. "Damn it!" He slapped the steering wheel. "You're making me crazy, Livvy."

"I'm sorry," she said. "I'll pay for the red light ticket." She laid her hand on his thigh. "You don't have to waste your time babysitting me. It's broad daylight. The El will be fine."

"First of all, I'm a cop. I won't get a fucking red light ticket." His tires screeched as he pulled to the curb and swiveled to face her. "I'm not *babysitting* you. You're capable of taking care of yourself. I know that. But..." He jerked his head toward her briefcase on the floor. "You carry a gun in there? And if so, do you know how to use it?"

"No. No gun." She wrapped her arms around herself, the thought of needing one making her stomach twist.

"Livvy, I don't want you going anywhere by yourself until we get this case under control." He slammed his hand on the steering wheel, making it wobble. "A guy was killed this morning because you were going to ask him about Bates. You've been asking a lot of questions about Anson. Where do you think that puts you on the 'people to get rid of' list?"

She sucked in a breath. "You're trying to scare me."

"Damn right I am. Is it working?"

Yes. It was. "Fine," she said. "Drop me off at the Daley Center Plaza."

He stared at her for a long minute. "You gonna call me when you're ready to leave?"

"Yes. I'll call you. I promise." She put her hand on his thigh and squeezed the hard muscles. "I get that this has gotten dangerous. But it's one thing to kill a low level dealer. I don't think they'll go after an assistant state's attorney. Bates knows what a shit storm that would cause."

"You think he won't go after you?" Ryan snorted. "Think again. Bates has been in Cook County Jail for a month, and he doesn't like it. He's getting desperate. Why do you think he hired a big dog attorney like Bennett?

"Now he's worried because you're finding the weak links in his chain. Screwing things up for him. If he thinks getting rid of you would derail the case against him, he wouldn't hesitate to send someone after you."

"I'm not the only ASA on this," she said, reaching for his hand. "There's a whole team of us working on the Bates case."

"But you're the one working with me." His voice gentled and he slid his fingers between hers. "You're the one who talked to Sampson and Williams. You're the most immediate threat. The most dangerous."

She stared at their joined hands, the connection sparking between them. She felt safe with Ryan. Protected. Why was she jabbing at him?

Finally she lifted her head and met his concerned gaze. "You're right, and I apologize. I'm not used to someone...taking care of me. Thinking about my safety."

"What kinds of assholes have you been dating?" he said, bringing their joined hands to his mouth to press a kiss to her wrist. Then he set them on his chest. His heart raced beneath her hand.

Dating. The word sent a frisson of anticipation through her. "Is that what we're doing? Dating?"

Flattening her hand against the hard wall of his chest, he held her gaze. "What would have happened last night if our pizza hadn't shown up when it did?"

Livvy drew in a deep, shuddering breath. She'd thought about that most of the night, the details unspooling in restless, erotic dreams. All featuring Ryan. "I don't think we would have had dinner," she whispered.

"You're right. Five more minutes, and neither of us would have heard your doorbell." He kissed her hand one more time, then let her go and pulled into traffic again. "So I think we're dating." He glanced at her, one side of his mouth curling up. "Even if we have to sneak around."

"Is that what you want?" she asked, disappointment crashing through her.

"Hell, no. But you said we couldn't get together because that high-priced attorney of Bates' would use it in court. So we're left with sneaking." He shot her another glance. "It's either that, or stay away from each other. Your choice."

Her heart fluttered. So did other parts of her. "Sneaking," she whispered. "Definitely sneaking. We're on the same side. It's not like we'll be passing secrets back and forth during pillow talk."

"Got news for you, babe." He pulled up to the curb at the Daley Center. "The only kind of pillow talk we'll have will be 'yes. More. That. Right there. Oh, God'." He grinned at her as he slid out of the car. "The only secrets I want to know are what revs your engine. Where you want me to touch you. And how loud you scream when you come."

He opened her car door, glanced around and held out his hand to help her out of the car. "Think about your answers. There'll be a test later."

She swallowed as they walked across the plaza, too turned on to speak. As she reached for the door to the building, his hand tightened on hers. "Call me when you're ready to leave. I'll pick you up right here."

"Okay," she managed to say. "I will."

He studied her face. His self-satisfied smirk told her he knew exactly how aroused she was. "I'll see you later, Livvy."

She stared at his mouth. "Looking forward to it."

"Me, too." He squeezed her hand, then let her go. He stood waiting as she walked inside. He was still there when her elevator door closed.

* * *

Livvy closed Gus Swenson's office door carefully, her hand gripping the doorknob tightly to prevent herself from slamming it. She wanted to make the walls shake with her fury. She wanted to tell Swenson exactly what she thought of him.

He'd told her to work harder. To get something solid against Bates. The connection between Philby's murder and Bates was too thin. It wouldn't hold up in court, especially with Henry Bennett defending Bates.

After fifteen minutes of negotiating, she'd managed to wring from Gus a promise of protective custody for

Williams and Sampson if they coughed up any useful information. But his dismissal of the rest of her efforts stung.

She stormed into her own office and sank into her chair. The last time she'd met with Swenson and gotten pissed off was after he'd assigned her to work with Ryan.

Some of her anger dissipated as she thought about how that had turned out. Gus's smug expression at that initial meeting told her the state's attorney had expected fireworks between her and Ryan. Lots of shouting and anger. Gus had been stirring the pot, hoping something would boil over.

Huh. Maybe Gus was shrewder than she'd realized. Something had boiled over, all right. And as a result, she and Ryan had put aside their history and actually worked together. They hadn't yet found the silver bullet that would take Bates down, but they were circling closer.

The personal connection they were forging? Gus wouldn't care about that.

But for the last couple of days, Livvy had spent a *lot* of time thinking about it.

Livvy swallowed, thinking about what might happen that evening. After Ryan picked her up.

She wasn't impulsive when it came to men. She went slowly. Cautiously. The debacle with James Dugger more than a month ago had been an aberration, and it had only reinforced her usual restraint. Fortunately, she'd caught him going through her briefcase before he could read the file she had on his buddy David Blaine.

She was falling for Ryan too quickly. She knew that. But he was different. He didn't want anything from her. They'd been forced together by Swenson. He was the last man she should be interested in, after what had happened between Ryan and Cilla, but he wasn't that man anymore.

He was protective of her. Thoughtful. Concerned about her safety.

And he made her pulse race and her heart pound like no

other man ever had.

Last night, he'd done nothing more than give her a foot massage, and she'd melted into a puddle on the couch. Spent all night thinking about the kiss they'd shared.

Shoving the images out of her mind, she grabbed a pen, opened a folder for a case she was taking to trial in a few weeks, and tried to put Ryan out of her mind. Mooning over him all day would only lead to frustration and clock-watching.

Hours later, when the second hand of her wall clock ticked over to five p.m., she tucked her pen into a drawer and pushed away from her desk. She'd glanced at the clock more than a few times in the past hour. Once or twice, she'd sworn it was broken.

Slipping the Bates file into her folder, she grabbed her phone and pushed Ryan's call icon as she walked into the hall. He answered after the first ring. Had he been watching the clock, too?

"Hey," he said, his voice soft. "You ready to go?"

"I'm heading for the elevator now."

"I'll be there in ten. Stay inside until you see my car."

"Okay." She swallowed. "See you soon, Ryan."

"Yeah. You will." His voice had dropped into the throaty rasp that made her skin prickle.

"'Bye," she murmured as she pressed the off icon.

The elevators were always slow at five in the afternoon, so it took several minutes for one to stop. When she made it to the first floor, she moved to a window to watch for Ryan.

There he was. Just east of Daley Plaza, stopped at the light on Randolph. First in a long row of cars.

Her heart pounding, she stepped out of the building and started across the wide pedestrian plaza toward the street. It was a no-parking zone, so Ryan could pull over, she'd jump into the car, and they'd be off.

The temperature had dropped since the morning, and a wet mixture of sleet and rain dampened her hair and coat.

The cement was slippery beneath her feet, slick with the slushy mixture.

As she stepped away from the shelter of the building, the wind howled around the corner, smacking her in the face with icy sleet pellets. Hunching her shoulders, she raised the collar of her coat to protect her neck from the weather. Her hands were already cold, so she shoved them into her pockets.

She glanced up for Ryan's car. The light hadn't yet turned. She should have waited a minute longer to leave the building, but she was eager to see him. Slide into his car and greet him.

Not with a kiss in front of so many eyes. But she could twine her fingers with his, press a kiss to his knuckles. Not nearly as satisfying, but it would have to do until they got to her place. Or his.

Maybe there was something to be said for sneaking around. It certainly built anticipation. Smiling, she looked up again to see his car inching through the intersection. Edging toward the curb in front of her.

She walked as quickly as she could toward him, startled when he leaped out of his car before he reached her, his door hanging open. Car horns blared and brakes shrieked as he sprinted toward her.

Someone to her right screamed. She turned to see a car jump the curb from Dearborn and race across the plaza, aimed straight at her in a blur of silver.

She froze for an instant, unable to comprehend what she saw, then she began to run. She'd chosen the wrong shoes for the weather, because the leather-soled pumps slid on the slick cement, not allowing her to get a good grip and take off.

The silver car veered toward her like a missile locked onto its target. It skidded, and Livvy took a deep breath. But the car's tires caught and it sped up again.

She wasn't going to make it to the car. The silver car was too close. She was too far from Ryan. She put her head down and ran. The engine revved. The tires growled against the pavement. Too close.

The heavy vibrations traveled up her legs through the pavement. She tried to run faster, knowing she wasn't going to make it. Determined to try anyway.

Exhaust fumes filled the air, and the roar of the engine was all she heard as she suddenly went flying through the air.

CHAPTER TEN

Skidding on the slippery pavement, his heart in his throat, Ryan grabbed Livvy's wrist hand and yanked her toward him as the car sped toward them. As his feet flew out from beneath him on the icy surface, he wrapped one arm around Livvy and used his other hand to protect her face.

He twisted as they toppled to the pavement, trying to cushion her impact with the hard cement. The back of his hand scraped over the icy slush and rough concrete, but Livvy's cheek and head were spared. Except for her chin. It hit the pavement with a dull thud as he tightened his hold on her.

The silver car flew past, so close he saw each individual splatter of ice on the sides. The icy, dirty slush that sprayed from its tires dripped into his eyes. His mouth. Over his scalp. Down the collar of his jacket.

People shouted in the distance. An approaching siren wailed. Livvy was motionless beneath him.

"Livvy." Ryan slid clumsily off her, knelt in the slush beside her. "Can you hear me, Liv?" He ran his hands over her back. Her arms. Touched her head. Froze when he saw the blood in front of her face, turning the slush on the pavement a dirty pink.

"Livvy! Are you okay?" Knowing the frantic fear in his voice would panic her, he tamped down the dread rushing through him. "Can you open your eyes, babe?"

Her eyes fluttered open. She stared at him, blinking. Confused. "Ryan? Did that car hit you, too?"

"No. It didn't hit either of us." He tucked a strand of wet, dirty hair out of her face. "An ambulance is on its way," he said, stroking her head. "Don't move, Liv. Lie still. Wait for the EMTs."

She frowned, studying his face. "Are you sure that car didn't hit me? I knew I wasn't going to make it."

"I got to you in time. Yanked you out of his way." He brushed his fingers along her forehead. Her nose. No bleeding there. "I thought I cushioned your head, but you hit somewhere. You're bleeding."

"I am?" She reached up to touch her face, and he tugged her hand down.

"Don't move. Please, babe." He curled his fingers around hers. "People are calling 911. An ambulance is on its way."

"Mouth hurts," she said, her tongue sliding along her lips. "Taste blood."

He leaned around her and saw the trickle of blood coming out of her mouth. "Yeah, your mouth is bleeding." He tightened the grip on her hand. "God, I'm so sorry, Liv. So sorry I hurt you."

She frowned at him, as if he was speaking a foreign language she didn't understand. "Didn't hurt me. Saved me."

He pressed a kiss to her forehead. "Hurt you in the process."

"So what?" She turned her palm and slid her fingers through his. Gripped tightly. "I'm alive, aren't I?"

"Yeah, you're alive." He exhaled, relief and adrenaline

washing through him, making him tremble. "Thank God."

"Want to see you," she said, trying to move her head.

Ryan held her gently in place. "Don't move. Wait for the ambulance."

"What happened to the car?"

"Disappeared." Rage flashed through him. Followed by helplessness. He wasn't used to crouching on the ground beside a victim. He was used to chasing down the bad guy.

Today, he wasn't budging from Livvy's side.

"Silver," she said. "It was silver."

"Yeah, it was." He swallowed, squeezing her hand more tightly. She was lying on the cold, hard, wet cement, and she'd remembered the car. She was so damn tough. "A lot of people were around. Maybe they got the license. Told the dispatchers where it went."

Livvy jumped at the sudden burp of a siren. Ryan put his hand on her back, holding her in place. "Don't move, okay? Stay as still as you can." The siren cut out and he spotted the flashing lights of an ambulance rounding the corner. "Bus is here."

A man stopped in front of them. Squatted down. "She okay?"

His black wingtips were covered in slush. The hems of his dark gray suit pants trailed in the icy mix, turning the fabric even darker. Gus Swenson.

Ryan tightened his grip on her hand. "Swenson. I think so. Car didn't hit her. I knocked her down."

Silence. "Good job, Ward," Swenson finally said. "Thanks. Olivia means a lot to all of us."

"No thanks necessary." Ryan's voice was cool. "Glad I was here."

"Let me know how she's doing."

"Will do, sir."

Swenson touched her head lightly, then stood and kept walking.

The bus stopped fifteen feet away. The doors flew open, and a female EMT grabbed a bag from the back of the bus and ran over. She squatted next to Livvy. "Call said she was hit by a car."

"No, thank God. I snatched her out of the way. But we hit the ground hard. Her mouth's bleeding. She said it hurt."

"She hit her head when you knocked her down her?"

"I don't think so. I tried to protect her head and face with my hand." He wiped a trickle of blood away from her mouth. "Obviously not completely, though."

"Sir! Don't touch her blood!" the EMT said sharply.

"It's okay," Ryan said, wiping another trickle from her chin. "She's my...I know her."

"We've got this," the EMT said. She didn't move. Neither did Ryan.

Finally, the woman touched his arm. "I know you're scared and upset, but you need to step back and let me assess her. The sooner we get her in the bus, the sooner she's on her way to the ER."

Ryan squeezed Livvy's hand. Lingered. He let her go, letting his fingers trail over her palm until they hit the cold sleet on the ground.

"Ryan?" Livvy's voice wavered.

He stepped around and squatted in front of her. Where she could see him. Some of the anxiety in her eyes dissipated. "I'm right here, Liv. Just giving the EMTs room to work."

Ten minutes later, they had her strapped to a back board, her neck in a brace. He squeezed her hand, then let her go as they boosted the gurney onto its wheels. The EMTs slid the gurney into the back of the ambulance and secured it. Before they could close the door, Ryan jumped inside.

"Sorry, sir. Only family can ride with us." The woman EMT's expression softened. She put her hand on Ryan's arm. "We're going to Northwestern, and you have to move your car. You're causing a huge back up. Why don't you meet us there?"

"I'm coming into the ER." Ryan wasn't asking, and the

EMT knew it.

After a long moment, the woman nodded. "I'll tell the nurses to watch for you. What's your name?"

"Ryan Ward." He glanced at her name tag. S. Ketchum. "Thank you, Ms. Ketchum."

"We'll see you there, Mr. Ward."

He bent down and brushed a kiss to Livvy's forehead. Squeezed her hand one more time. "I'm right behind you, babe."

"Promise?" Livvy clung to him for a moment, then let him go when he nodded. "Okay. Thanks."

The doors slammed, and Ryan stood in the sleet and watched the bus begin to move. It bumped over the curb, sirens wailing, and wove in and out of the cars.

Livvy was in there, immobilized by the backboard and neck brace. Worrying about possible injuries. Disoriented because she couldn't move, couldn't see anything but the ceiling of the bus. She'd slide a little from side to side as the ambulance turned, but she'd have no warning.

He watched until the bus disappeared, then raced for his car. He threw up the gumball and lit it up. Began weaving between cars and taxis and buses. He was damn well going to make it to that hospital as fast as he could. He'd promised Livvy. She needed him.

Ten minutes later, he stood in front of the triage nurse at Northwestern's emergency room. "Olivia Marini. She was just brought in."

"Have a seat, sir," the nurse said, her eyes weary. "We'll let you know when you can go in."

Ryan unclipped his badge from his belt and held it up. "Chicago PD. I need to get back there. I followed the ambulance in."

Pursing her lips, the nurse pulled up a screen on the computer. Studied it for what seemed like hours. Finally she nodded. "Ms. Marini is in room R. Through those doors and to your left."

Ryan glanced at her name tag. "Thank you, Ms. Evans."

"Hope she's okay," the nurse said as she pushed a button to open the ER door.

Ryan nodded. "Thanks."

He strode down the hall of the emergency room, ignoring the beeping machines, the crying people, the soothing voices of the nurses. When he arrived at Room R, the curtain was pulled in front of the door. He reached to pull it aside. Stopped when he heard Livvy's voice.

"Hey! Why did you cut off my pants? I hurt my head, not my legs."

Ryan's hand on the curtain relaxed. If she was complaining about losing her clothes, she couldn't be too badly hurt.

"We need to check you out," a kind voice said. "Standard procedure in an ER starts with getting rid of the clothes."

"Those were my favorite pants," Livvy said, her voice sulky.

He'd buy her a new pair. As soon as she was out of here.

He knocked on the glass window in front of the curtain, and a nurse stuck her head out. "Who are you?"

"Ryan Ward. I'm with Ms. Marini."

She studied him for a long moment, then glanced over her shoulder. "They're getting her into a gown and starting her IV," she said to him. "I'll let you know when you can come in."

He stood in the hall, his hands shoved into his pockets, his toe tapping the floor. It felt like hours, but it was probably only minutes before the nurse eased the curtain to the side for him.

"Stay out of our way," she ordered. "Let her know you're here, then stand in the corner. If you don't cooperate, you're out of here."

"Got it," he said. "Will do. And thank you. I know you don't have to do this."

Her fierce expression eased. "She's waiting for you, too."

The nurse stepped aside, and Ryan spotted Livvy, lying in the bed, covered with a blanket. Wires and tubes snaked out from beneath it, attached to machines and bags of liquids. Livvy's face was pale against the white pillow, and her eyes were closed.

"Hey, Liv," he said, stepping close to her head.

Her eyes fluttered open. "Ryan?"

"Yeah. I'm here." He reached under the blanket until he found her hand, then carefully slid his palm beneath hers. "How are you feeling?"

"Fine. I feel goood." She blinked at him, her eyes drifting in and out of focus. "Are you fine, too?"

"I am. Looks like they gave you the good drugs, and I'm guessing your head doesn't hurt anymore," he said, the corners of his mouth fighting a smile. "So I have no complaints."

"*I* have a complaint." She scowled. "They cut off my clothes. *All* of them. Including my favorite work pants. So no peeking."

"Not even a little?" He tickled her palm with his fingers. "How about your legs? Can I peek at those? Or your arms?"

She frowned, her eyebrows squinching together. "No! You can peek later. When we're at home."

At home. A week ago, those words would have sent him running. Scrambling to get as far away as possible.

Now? A tiny tremor vibrated in his chest. He refused to call it want. Anticipation, maybe. Eagerness.

Not want.

"You're right," he said, trying to keep his voice light. "I don't want anyone else around the first time I see you naked."

A nurse nudged him aside. "You need to step out of the room," she said briskly. "We're going to take some x-rays."

Ryan started to move away, and Livvy grabbed for his hand. "Don't go."

"It's just for a few minutes, Liv. I'll be right outside the door. And as soon as it's safe, I'll be back in." He watched as a tech rolled a lumbering x-ray machine into place. "You want me to call your sister?"

Livvy mumbled a string of numbers. "Tell her I'm okay. Not to come to the hospital. Then you'll come back?"

"I will."

"Promise?" Her hand tightened on his as he gently tugged his fingers away.

"I promise. I'm not leaving."

"Good," she breathed, staring up at him.

"I won't leave your side as long as you're in the hospital. Okay?"

"Okay," she said, letting her eyes drift closed.

* * *

Livvy leaned heavily against him as they walked up the stairs to her apartment. She stumbled frequently, but he'd been prepared and held her steady. The doctor had warned him the painkillers would take several hours to dissipate.

The smell of the mac and cheese he'd picked up from Oscar's swirled around them, reminding him how hungry he was. She'd said she wanted to eat, but she'd said a lot of stuff on the way home. Most of which had made him blush. And turned him on.

He'd had to pull his shirt out of his jeans when he walked into Oscars. Like he was nineteen damn years old and unable to control himself.

He fumbled in her briefcase for her keys, unlocked the door, and helped her inside. "You want to sit on the couch? I'll serve up the mac and cheese."

"Couch is good." She stared up at him, her eyes bleary. "Good memories on this couch."

"Yeah? What would those be?"

She nudged his shoulder. "You were there. You forgot already?"

Memories of that evening had scrolled through his head

ever since. "Haven't forgotten anything." He touched her cheek. "Those are good memories."

He eased her onto the couch and put a throw pillow behind her head. "I'll be right back," he said. "Close your eyes and relax. Okay?"

"Okay." She nodded, her head bouncing gently up and down. She looked like one of those bobble-head dolls they passed out at Blackhawk's games.

He arranged her head on the pillow. "We'll have some food, then you can lie down."

When he returned with two plates and a glass of water for her, Livvy's eyes were closed. He sat next to her, and the movement of the cushion had her opening her eyes and gazing at him.

"You're still here." She gave him a brilliant, tipsy smile.

"With food," he said, handing her a plate.

The macaroni and cheese with bacon and spinach was delicious. Exactly what he needed – comfort food to the max. Livvy ate most of hers, but after a while her hand began to tremble, the tines of the fork clinking on the plate.

"Had enough?" he asked, taking it away from her.

"S'good," she managed to say. She swayed a little when she turned to look at him. "I'll call you tomorrow. 'Kay?"

"Hey." The couch dipped as he slid closer. "I'm not going anywhere. If you have a spare bedroom, I'll sleep in there. Otherwise, the couch is fine."

She blinked, forcing her eyes open. "You'll stay?"

He narrowed his eyes. "Of course I'll stay. Unless you'd rather have someone else," he said, ignoring the disappointment churning through him. "Your sister said she'd come over and stay with you."

"I'd rather have you. And sex." She swayed toward him. "Can we have sex, Ryno?"

Ryno? He swallowed his snort of laughter. "I don't think sex is on the agenda tonight, Liv. I want you completely awake and aware when we make love."

He froze at the words that slipped out of his mouth. *Sex.*

That's what they were talking about. Not making love. It would be sex. Fun. Nothing more.

"I am awake. And I want sex tonight." She reached for him and her hand slipped off his thigh. "You promised."

His mouth twitched and the panic faded. It had been a long day. No wonder he was confused. "We'll have sex when you're feeling better. Come on, Loopy Livvy. Let's get you to bed."

He helped her off the couch, and she stumbled into the bathroom. When she swayed in front of the sink, Ryan held her waist as she brushed her teeth. Then he guided her into her bedroom.

Although it was dark, with only slats of moonlight illuminating the room, it was as colorful and comfortable as the rest of her apartment. He steered her toward her bed, helping her sit as she staggered against him.

"You want pajamas?" he asked.

"You going to help me change? No one else here to see me naked." She tried to press a kiss to his neck, but stumbled against him.

God! Even with the drugs, she'd remembered what he said in the ER.

Arousal swept over him in a dark, heavy wave. Livvy stared at him, desire filling her eyes, and he curled his hand around her upper arm. "On second thought? The scrubs will work just fine."

Holding her with one arm, he threw the quilt, blanket and top sheet back, then eased her down onto the bed. Livvy rubbed at the bandage covering the road rash on her chin, then curled onto her side. "You're staying?" she asked, watching him.

"Right next door in your spare room," he assured her.

"No." Livvy frowned. "In here. You said you'd stay."

"You want me to sleep in your bed with you?" He shoved his hand through his hair. Damn.

"Yes," she said, smiling as if pleased he'd finally gotten it.

He wanted to curl around her. Keep her safe. But she was drugged. "You sure, Loopy Livvy?"

"Yes. I'm sure." She waved a hand at him. "Take off your clothes."

"You're bossy when you're drugged up," he said, unable to stop the tiny smile.

As she watched, he unbuttoned his shirt and laid it over a chair. Did the same with his jeans. Then he slid into bed beside her in his boxer briefs and tee shirt.

"The doctor told me someone needed to wake you up a couple of times during the night," he said, staying a careful foot away from her. "You don't have any signs of a concussion, but he wants to make sure there isn't a slow bleed in your head."

"You can wake me up anytime you want," she said, wriggling across the bed until she was right next to him.

"Go to sleep, babe," he whispered. He should keep his distance. But with her curled trustingly against him, he couldn't let her go. He drew her back against his chest. She felt perfect nestled against him, her body warm and soft against his. He wrapped an arm around her abdomen and snugged her closer. "I'll be right here in case you have bad dreams."

She relaxed into him. "Won't dream about that car," she whispered, so softly that he could barely hear her. "Even in my dreams, you won't let it run me down."

CHAPTER ELEVEN

Livvy licked her lips, squinting in the sunlight that sneaked through the slats of her blinds. Her mouth felt as if the entire French army had marched through it during the night.

She needed water.

Still half asleep, she stumbled out of bed and staggered into the bathroom, wincing at the sharp ache in her left leg and arm. She splashed water into a paper cup and drank. Filled it twice more before she felt close to human.

Tossing the cup into the trash, she caught sight of herself in the mirror. A white bandage covered her chin. Her lip was swollen, her hair tangled. She leaned closer. There was actual *dirt* in it. She wore blue pajamas that weren't hers.

They were hospital scrubs, she realized as she glanced down at them.

Everything that had happened the day before came roaring back. Philby dead. The car speeding across Daley plaza. Ryan yanking her out of its way, tackling her to the ground. The emergency room.

Her memory was fuzzy after that. Ryan had brought her

home. They'd eaten…something. He'd tucked her into bed.

She'd asked him to stay. To sleep in the bed with her.

Heat swept over her body as vague memories stirred. She'd asked him for more than that.

Hurrying back into her bedroom, she found indentations on both of her pillows. The covers on the other side of the bed were rumpled. Folded over, as if someone had tossed them aside.

Not someone. Ryan.

He'd stayed, just as she'd asked. Slept in her bed, too.

Disappeared before she woke up.

Disappointment, sharp and bitter, stung the back of her throat. She'd thought they were becoming… Her mind refused to name it. More than colleagues, though. More than two people forced to work together.

Dropping the scrubs on the floor, she turned on the shower. Waited until the water was hot, then stepped beneath the spray.

Fifteen minutes later, she stepped out of the tub, clean and feeling much better. She'd even managed to keep the bandage on her chin dry. As she toweled her hair, she heard her front door open. Close. Softly, as if whoever entered was trying to be quiet.

Ryan's words played in her head. *Where do you think you are on Bates' 'people to get rid of' list?*

Hands shaking, she wrapped herself in the towel. Tried twice before she managed to knot it between her breasts.

Livvy yanked open a drawer, scrabbling for anything that could be used as a weapon. Combs. A hairbrush. A handful of Q-tips. An eyebrow pencil. Tiny cases of eye shadow. Mascara. A tweezer.

A pointy tweezer. Clutching her pitiful weapon tightly, she eased the bathroom door open.

Rattling sounds drifted out of the kitchen. Was he searching for something?

Tip-toeing through the dining room, holding the towel

109

against her chest, she stopped at the kitchen door. Inhaled once, shakily. Again.

Stepped around the corner, the tweezers extended stiffly in front of her.

"Ryan?"

He turned, smiling at her. "Liv. How do you…" His smile disappeared when he saw the tweezers clutched between her thumb and index finger. Noticed her hand shaking as she pointed them at him.

"Hey." He closed his hand around hers, tugged the tweezers away. Tossed them onto the counter, then folded her into his arms. "How are you feeling this morning?"

She shoved at his chest until he let her go. "I'm feeling pissed off. 'Almost wet my pants' scared. Wondering why you're here." She shoved him again, but instead of backing up, he closed his fingers around hers and pressed her palm against his chest.

He curled his other arm around her waist and drew her closer. "What's this about, Livvy?"

Staring at his hand covering hers, feeling his heart racing beneath her palm, she closed her eyes and took a deep breath. "You left." She wanted to press a kiss to his hand, but wouldn't let him know how…destroyed she'd felt. "I thought you were gone. I heard someone open the door. I thought…I thought I was the next one on Bates' list."

He let her hand go, wrapped both arms around her and pulled her close. "I'm sorry, babe. I didn't leave you. I couldn't…*wouldn't* do that. I didn't want to wake you, so I went downstairs to call your sister. I told her you were still asleep, but you didn't have any concussion symptoms when I woke you up." He stroked his hand down her wet hair, again and again, and her fear and anger faded as tears trickled down her cheeks. "Figured I could make it to Della's and back while you were still asleep."

He eased away from her and brushed wet strands of hair away from her face. "I wanted to be here when you woke up. But you were zonked out. After yesterday, I figured you'd sleep a lot longer."

Livvy took a deep, shuddering breath. Inhaled his fresh air and sunshine scent. Wiped her damp cheeks against his shirt. "'S okay," she murmured into his chest. "I over-reacted. I'm sorry."

His arms tightened around her. "I shouldn't have gone to Della's." His hard body was warm against hers. Comforting.

He made her feel safe.

"Give me some coffee and we're good," she said. Instead of moving, she pressed closer against him. Forgot about her sore chin, her fat lip, the ache in her arms and legs. Ryan was solid. Real. She wanted to stay wrapped around him forever.

"Coffee's right here," he said. He didn't let her go, though.

Coffee would reheat. Ignoring the sting in her lip, she lifted her face, stood on tiptoe and pressed her mouth to his. He hesitated for a long moment, framing her face with his hands. But when she wound her arms around his neck, his eyes fluttered closed. He pressed his lips softly against hers, careful to avoid the puffy, sore spot. "Liv," he murmured against her mouth.

"You made a promise last night." She touched his lips with her tongue, desire licking through her body like flames. "Wasn't so drugged up I forgot that."

"Yeah. I did." He ran his hands down her sides, pressed her hips closer to his. "I'm not sure you're feeling better, though. I saw you limping."

"Never thought I'd have to beg you to have sex with me." She pressed her hips into his, felt the satisfying weight of his erection against her. He wanted her, too.

"God, Livvy," he groaned, burying his face in her neck. "You're making me crazy. You need to get dressed before I do something I shouldn't do." He tucked in her knotted towel more firmly.

"You're right. I shouldn't be wearing this towel. I'll take

it off." Her hands shook as she reached for the knot, and his fingers closed over hers.

"Not exactly what I meant, babe."

They stared at each other, his hand holding the towel in place as she tried to loosen it. The sudden buzz of her doorbell was a splash of icy water to her libido.

Ryan's, too. Desire disappeared from his eyes, replaced by hard determination. His hands fell away from her. The softness vanished from his eyes. "Go get dressed." His fingers hovered over the gun at his hip. "I'll see who's at the door."

He nodded toward her bedroom. "Stay there until I tell you it's okay to come out."

She backed away from him, holding his gaze as she clutched the knot on the towel. He watched until she was out of sight in the bedroom. Then he moved. The old hardwood floor creaked as he headed toward the front door. The whisper of metal against leather drifted toward her. He'd drawn his gun from its holster

Letting the towel drop to the floor, she threw on a tee shirt and pair of yoga pants. Warm socks. Even the sweater she pulled on over the tee shirt couldn't stop her violent shivering.

"Yes?" His voice carried menace. Warning.

The reply was hard to hear from her bedroom. She heard the locks on the door click open, though. She walked out of her bedroom, then froze, remembering Ryan's last words. *"Stay there until I tell you it's okay to come out."*

She peeked around the corner. Ryan stood at the door, his gun in his hand.

Swallowing hard, she backed into her bedroom. Stood at the door, listening.

The door creaked open. "Ward?" Cilla's voice. "What the hell are you doing here?"

* * *

"Looking out for your sister." Ryan held Cilla's gaze, refusing to back down. She didn't get to make him feel as if he didn't belong here. Livvy had asked him to stay.

As he held Cilla's gaze, he heard footsteps behind him. Livvy. Wincing as she approached them.

"Cill," Livvy said with a sob of relief.

She'd begged him to stay last night. Said she'd wanted to have sex with him. Had she really wanted her sister to stay, instead? Had she let him stay out of some damn misguided 'thank you for saving me' shit?

Cilla push past Ryan and enveloped Livvy in a tight hug. Held her for a long moment. Then eased away.

"How are you feeling?" she asked softly, brushing Livvy's hair out of her face.

Livvy raised one shoulder. "Fine. Basically." Her gaze flickered to his, then away. "Thanks to Ryan."

Cilla frowned. "What do you mean, 'thanks to Ryan?'"

"He didn't tell you when he called?"

"He said you'd had an accident. You were in the ER. That you were sore, but otherwise okay. That's it." She narrowed her gaze at Ryan. "Other than I shouldn't come to the hospital."

Livvy sucked her lower lip into her mouth. Let it pop out again. "Come sit down, Cill. I'm a little sore."

Ryan leaned against the door, watching them. He felt like a third wheel. Unnecessary. In the way. Someone they were merely tolerating.

Livvy lowered herself carefully onto the couch, and Cilla sat next to her. Took Livvy's hand, held it tightly between hers. "Tell me what happened."

Cilla was going to try and toss him out of Livvy's apartment. Ryan could read it in her body language – she was practically draped over her sister. Protecting her. From him?

His jaw clenching, he watched the two heads so close together. Both of them with those thick waves of whiskey-colored hair. From the side, so similar, they could be twins.

113

Blood always trumped friends.

The thought hollowed him out, and he pushed away from the door. He'd get his damn coffee. Leave Livvy and her sister alone.

"Where are you going, Ryan?" Livvy's voice.

He glanced over his shoulder. "To get my coffee."

She studied him for a long moment, as if she could see the coldness enveloping him. "Would you get mine, too, please?" she asked softly.

"Sure," he said, swallowing. Maybe she *didn't* want him banished to the kitchen.

When he returned to the living room, Livvy had leaned against the back of the couch. Cilla sat right beside her, still holding her hand. Ryan set her coffee on the table in front of the two women, then sat in the chair across from them.

Livvy watched him over the rim of the coffee cup, then set it down on the table. "Scoot over, Cill," she said nudging her sister with her hip.

Cilla frowned, but she moved away from Livvy.

"More," Livvy said.

Cilla retreated all the way to the other end of the couch, and Livvy scooted after her. Patting the cushion on her other side, she said, "C'mere, Ryan."

As soon as he lowered himself onto the sofa, she took his hand. It was hard to miss Cilla's sudden frown.

Her gaze drifted from Livvy's face to his, but she didn't say a word. Finally Cilla said to Livvy, "Tell me what happened."

"A car tried to run me down in Daley Plaza," she said. Her voice held little emotion, as if she was merely reciting facts. Then her expression softened as she gazed at him. "Ryan pulled me out of the way. We hit the pavement hard, and I ended up with a few bruises and a scraped chin. Cut mouth. That's it." The unspoken 'could have been so much worse' hung in the air between them.

"What?" Cilla bounced to her feet, her gaze shifting between Livvy and Ryan. "What the hell is going on?"

"Bates is getting worried," Ryan said. Livvy leaned against him. He wanted to wrap his arm around her, but clenched his fist on his thigh instead. Cilla was already unhappy with his presence in her sister's apartment.

Livvy squirmed her fingers between his arm and his chest and curled her hand around his biceps.

The ice inside him began to melt.

He cleared his throat. "I'm pretty sure the car that almost hit Livvy is the same one that's been following me for a few days."

"Are you putting my sister in danger, Ward?" Cilla demanded.

He was, damn it all to hell. And there wasn't a fucking thing he could do about it. "Anyone I worked with would be in danger." He tried to keep the anger out of his voice. "That's on Bates. Who do you think is behind that silver car that almost hit your sister? The black car following her?"

"That *bastard*." Cilla straightened. "What can we do?"

The damn Donovans couldn't do any more than he was already doing. "I'm going to visit Bates in Cook County Jail," Ryan said. "Act like I'm on his side. See if I can get anything out of him."

Livvy shifted to face him, frowning. But still holding onto him. "Do you think he'll believe you're on his side? Given that you're working with me?"

Ryan shrugged. "I'm sure he also knows that Swenson pretty much forced me to do it."

"He...you visited him at least once before." Livvy tightened her hand on his arm. "Don't you think he'll be suspicious when you show up now?"

It had only been there for a moment, but he'd seen the doubt in Livvy's expression. "Why do you think I visited him that time?"

"I have no idea."

He shifted subtly. Just enough to dislodge her hand from his arm. Enough to ensure they were no longer touching from knee to shoulder. "I asked him if his wife and kids were okay. If they needed anything." He rolled his shoulders, careful not to touch her. "He was a criminal, and he deserved to be in jail. His kids are innocent."

Livvy swiveled to face him on the couch. Grabbed his hands and held on, even when he tried to pull away. "All I meant was, if you made it clear you thought he was guilty a few weeks ago, he'll be suspicious if you're suddenly on his side."

He studied her for a long moment, and all he saw was concern. For his safety. The vise around his heart loosened.

"Do you think I don't trust you?" she said softly. He didn't miss the hurt in her voice.

"Do you?" he asked softly.

"Of course I do." The words were out almost before he'd finished speaking. "I just…I don't want him to put a target on you, too."

He relaxed his shoulders. Let out a breath. "News flash, babe. It's already there. I'm the guy who worked with him every day. The guy who knows him better than anyone else in the department. He probably thinks I know a lot more than I do."

Cilla leaned forward. "How much *do* you know, Ward?"

She still didn't trust him with her sister. He clenched his teeth. Deliberately relaxed. "Not nearly enough." He stared at his hands. "If they have any witnesses, or a dirtbag who's cooperating, I'd probably remember if Bates met with him or her. I've found some inconsistencies in the reports he wrote. Things he omitted. Changed. But I haven't found a smoking gun. Right now, I'm focused on protecting Livvy."

"We're all going to protect Livvy." Cilla continued to stare at Ryan, as if daring him to assert his claim on her.

He had no claim. He knew it. Cilla did, too. But he was staking one anyway. "That's good. Livvy and I can use all the help we can get."

"*You and Livvy*? Is that right, Ward?" Cilla narrowed her eyes at him.

He stared back. "That's right," he said softly.

"Maybe Williams or Sampson will come up with something." Livvy's voice was too loud, as if she was trying to break the tension vibrating between her sister and her...lover?

Not quite yet. But soon.

"Yeah. Maybe those two dirtbags will deliver the goods on Bates." Cilla's gaze flicked between Livvy and Ward. "In the meantime, I came over to take care of Livvy. So you don't have to stay, Ward."

"You're welcome to stay, of course," Ryan said. "But I'm not going anywhere."

Livvy gripped Ryan's hands tightly, then swiveled to face her sister. "You don't have to stay, Cill. I'm fine with Ryan."

Cilla studied Ryan for a long moment. "You sure?"

"Positive," Livvy answered.

Cilla stood slowly, her jaw tight. "I'll get going, then." She turned to Ryan. "You call me if anything changes. If you need anything. I can be here in less than fifteen minutes."

Ryan stood, as well. "Of course, Cilla. And thank you. I'll call if anything changes. I'll call if I have to go out. I'm not leaving Livvy alone."

"You don't call?" She pointed a finger at him. "I'll take you apart." Cilla reached out and pulled Livvy into a hug. "Take it easy, Liv. Feel better. I'll call you later."

Cilla walked out the door and Ryan locked it behind her. Then he edged a blind to the side. Livvy leaned against him, watching her sister get into her car.

Ryan let the blind drop. "Please go sit on the couch," he said quietly. "Now," he added as she hesitated.

Swallowing, Livvy stumbled to the couch and dropped onto it. Once she was seated, Ryan eased the blind to the side again. After a few moments, he let it drop.

"Cilla's gone. No one followed her. She knows to look for a tail on her way home."

"Is my sister in danger?" Livvy demanded.

He lifted one shoulder. "Maybe, since she's the one who arrested Bates. But probably no more than anyone else connected to this case. And Donovan will take care of her."

He dropped onto the couch beside her and reached for her hand. "That's why I'm going to see Anson in Cook County Jail. We need more information. Something we can use to keep him locked up. I don't want any more people hurt because of him."

"What was all that staring between you and Cilla?"

A smile curled one corner of his mouth. "She was telling me she'll rip my heart out of my chest if I hurt you. I was assuring her that I wouldn't do that. That you and I are on the same page."

"What page would that be?" Livvy asked, swinging her legs over his thighs and wriggling into his lap.

"The 'I'm going to keep you so close that Bates won't have a chance to hurt you' page. I was letting her know that keeping you safe is my only priority."

"Really?" She slid her fingers in between the buttons of his shirt, tangling them in his chest hairs. Her touch sent sparks shooting to his groin. "That's your only priority?"

He shifted beneath her, trying to focus on her words. "What else did you have in mind?"

"Mmm." She swung one leg over his lap so she was facing him, her thighs straddling his. Based on the way her eyelids fluttered close, his erection was pressing exactly where she needed it. "Promises were made yesterday," she murmured into the skin beneath his ear. "There was talk of nakedness."

"You were almost hit by a car," he said, smoothing his thumb over her swollen lip. He kissed the bandage on her chin. "You're beaten up. Having you feeling better is more important than nakedness."

"You ever hear of multi-tasking?" She slid both hands beneath his shirt, and his muscles jumped as if her fingers carried an electric current. "I think being naked would make me feel a whole lot better."

He tugged her hands from beneath his shirt and kissed one palm, then the other. "I know you're sore. I saw you limping. I don't want to hurt you, Livvy."

"Then we won't knock any lamps onto the floor or rip the sheets off the bed." She gave him a sly grin from beneath her eyelashes. "We'll save that for another time." She pressed her mouth to his and kissed him deeply. His heart thundering in his chest, he teased his tongue along the seam of her lips. Opening to him, she whispered into his mouth, "Make love with me, Ryan."

CHAPTER TWELVE

R yan's mouth stilled on hers, then he shifted. Before she could whimper at the loss of his body against hers, he swung her into the air, still kissing her. Livvy clutched his shoulders, and he curled her into his chest as if she were precious. Fragile.

Beloved.

She melted into him, her heart thrashing in her chest. That was exactly how she felt about Ryan.

"I can walk," she murmured into his mouth. She didn't want to walk. Holding her against his chest, Ryan made her feel cherished. Protected.

Never before had she wanted a man to protect her. But with Ryan, it was sexy. Arousing. Impossible to resist.

"I like carrying you." He brushed his cheek against hers, his scruff rough against her skin. "Like having you in my arms."

"Mmm." She ran her fingers over his chin, loving the scrape of the bristles on her fingertips.

"I have to conserve your strength," he said, nibbling at her earlobe as he angled her through the bedroom door.

"Don't want to wear you out."

"I'm all in favor of being worn out," she said, unbuttoning his shirt as he laid her on the bed.

The tails of his shirt fluttering at his sides, he shed his jeans and crawled onto the bed with her. Knelt on the mattress as he studied her. His eyes were dark, only a tiny rim of silver left. "You're so strong," he whispered. "So tough. And beautiful, too. You're perfect, Livvy."

The last tiny bit of her heart he didn't already own fell into his hands. "No, I'm not," she said, cupping his face in her hands to draw him closer. "But I want to be perfect for you."

"You are." His hands trembled and he paused as he drew her sweater over her head. He stared down at her, her thin tee shirt barely hiding her breasts. His skin tightened on his face and a flush crept up his neck. "Absolutely perfect."

She tossed the sweater to the floor and the movement made her tee shirt scrape over her too-sensitive nipples. She closed her eyes and fumbled for Ryan's hands, putting them on her chest. "Touch me, Ryan. Please," she begged.

Through her thin tee, his hands were hot. Gentle. She sucked in a breath and pressed up into his palms, her hands scrabbling at the waist of his boxer briefs. "I want to touch you, too."

As she slid her hands beneath his waistband, the stretchy material pressed her palms against his hard ass. His muscles flexed beneath her fingers, and he stilled above her. She tugged the material over his impressive erection, letting it gather at his knees, then sat up and pressed a kiss to his belly button.

She kissed her way down his abdomen, savoring the salty, clean taste of his skin. Tension vibrated off him as his muscles twitched beneath her mouth.

Before she reached her target, he eased her onto the bed. "No way," he said. "Not now. I'll go off like a firecracker if you go any farther."

He lifted her tee shirt, and cool air trailed over her torso. Drinking her in, he tossed her shirt onto the floor, yanked off his shorts and sank onto the bed. "So soft," he breathed, touching one nipple gently. It tightened beneath his finger, sending bolts of lightning through her body.

"My turn to play," he said, tugging off her yoga pants. He sat back on his heels and smiled down at her now-naked body. "Commando, Liv? I like it."

"Was kind of in a hurry," she said, shaking, as she reached for him.

"No hurry now," he murmured, taking her mouth. He kissed her slowly, exploring her face, her neck, the sensitive spot beneath her ear. She panted beneath him, her arousal making her tremble, her climax already building. He continued to move excruciatingly slowly. He clearly had far more self-control than she did.

Finally he slid his tongue along the seam of her lips, and she moaned with relief. As their tongues played, he trailed his hand along her side, making her wriggle. "Ticklish?" he murmured, leaving her mouth to explore the spot he'd found.

When she was squirming beneath him, he moved higher until he reached her breast. He suckled her skin, nipping and then soothing it. She grabbed his hair, trying to lead him where she wanted him, but he wouldn't budge. "Playing here," he murmured against her skin.

Finally, when she was certain she couldn't bear it any longer, he ran his tongue around her nipple. Then blew on it. The sensation of hot, then cold made her levitate off the bed. "Ryan," she gasped.

"Hmm?" he hummed as he sucked on her nipple.

"Oh, God." He lifted his head, and she grabbed his ears to hold him in place. "Don't stop," she begged.

"Never stopping," he said.

He froze for a moment, then slid lower, trailing tiny kisses along her abdomen. He put his mouth on her and sucked, and every cell in her body clenched. When he pressed the flat of his tongue against her, she exploded, screaming.

Ryan grabbed his jeans and pulled a foil packet out of his wallet. He fumbled the condom out of the package, sheathed himself, then slid into her.

They fit together perfectly. As if they were made for each other. When he began to move, she lifted her hips into him. Her skin tingled wherever it pressed against his. In moments she was climbing again. And when she came the second time, he was right with her.

He lowered himself onto her chest, wrapping his arms around her and nuzzling her neck. After a moment, he rolled so she was lying on top of him. Her heart was still racing. Her arms and legs trembled. She closed her eyes, listening to his heart pounding beneath her ear, and tunneled her hands into his hair.

"You okay?" he murmured into her hair.

"Amazing. You?" she managed to say.

"I'm…wow. Just…wow."

Livvy rubbed her cheek against his chest, his fine hairs tickling her nose. "Yeah. Wow sounds about right."

"I didn't hurt you, did I?" He tightened his arms around her. "I know you're still sore."

"I don't think so. I can't feel my arms and legs, though, so who knows?" She tried to burrow closer. "I guess we'll have to do that all over again if we want to find out."

He settled her against his side, then slid off the bed. "Hold that thought. I'll be right back."

She lay sprawled on the bed while he was in the bathroom, listening to him move around. Run water in the sink. Finally he slid into bed beside her. "C'mere," he said into her hair as he lifted her back onto his chest. Then he yanked the covers over their tangled-together bodies.

He inhaled deeply, and her heart melted into a gooey mess. To hide it, she asked, "Are you smelling my hair?"

"Mmm, yeah," he said, his voice dreamy. "You smell like oranges."

"You smell like sunshine," she said, rubbing her nose along his chest. She could lie here happily forever, holding Ryan. Touching him. Learning his body with her hands.

One of her legs nestled between his. As she tip-toed her fingers along his ribs, testing the shape of them, she felt him stir.

"Really?" she said, rising on one elbow to lick at one of his flat nipples. "Already?"

"What can I say?" He pillowed his head on his arms and watched her, his eyes droopy, his expression soft. "You have magical powers."

"You going to do something about it?"

"Thinking about it."

She wriggled her way down his body. "Keep thinking. It's my turn to play."

* * *

Finally, when the sky was purpling outside the window, Ryan sat up. Livvy lay beside him, her hair a tangled mess, one leg thrown over his, her body limp. His heart contracted as he watched the rise and fall of her chest as she breathed.

She was an adventurous lover, sexy, fun, and oh, so generous. He wanted to gather her close and never let go.

Before he could give in and wrap himself around her, he slid out of her bed.

"Hey," she said, her voice raspy and deep. "Where are you going?"

He smiled and leaned over to press a kiss into her hair. He'd been responsible for the screaming orgasms that had wrecked her voice. And there had been a lot of them. "Going to order some food. You need to keep up your strength."

Livvy rolled onto her back and smiled up at him. "I like the way you think."

He twitched the sheet over her amazing body to keep

himself from climbing back into the bed with her. "What do you want?"

"Hmm." Her eyes fluttered closed and her mouth curved into a dreamy smile. "You're good at surprising me. Surprise me again."

He ignored his cock's eager twitch. "Anything you don't like?"

"Not a huge fan of German food. But if you love it, order it."

"I'll be right back." He padded out of the room, glancing over his shoulder to find her watching him walk away. His cock swelled and he looked away, trying to ignore the rush of arousal.

He grabbed his phone and stared at his contact list, unable to think about anything but the woman in the next room. Finally he pushed the call icon next to his favorite pizza place. They'd have to discuss their preferred take-out joints.

Lot of other things they had to discuss, too. Like this case.

There was the splash of cold water he needed.

He should have been working. They needed to nail down this case against Anson, and they'd spent most of the day in bed instead.

"Tortello's," Mona's cheerful voice said.

"Hey, Mona, this is Ryan Ward. I'd like to order a pizza," he said.

"Your usual? Delivered to your address?"

"No. Large pepperoni and mushroom. And deliver it to this address." He recited Livvy's address. "Thanks, Mona."

"Early for you to be ordering. And a new address. You have something to share with the class, Ryan?"

Did he? A small flutter of warning vibrated in his head. He was too blissed out in the afterglow of amazing sex to care.

"Nothing I'm gonna share with you, you nosy woman."

Mona's deep laugh filled his ear. "Bring her in for dinner one of these days. If you can manage to get out of bed."

The blush scorched his body. Mona was old enough to be his mother. "Yeah, yeah, Mona. Thanks." He disconnected before the woman could say anything else.

Before heading back to the bedroom, he stepped into the living room, dark now with the approaching dusk. Teasing back the blinds, he searched the street for either the dirty silver car or the black one with the matte hood. He didn't spot either of them.

The blind fell back into place as he walked back to Livvy. Maybe Bates had a new guy watching him.

He'd rather have seen one of the old ones. At least then, he'd know who was out there.

He'd worry about it tomorrow. Today, all he could think about was Livvy.

* * *

Even before he opened his eyes, the light on his eyelids told Ryan he'd screwed up. It had been twenty-four hours since he carried Livvy to bed. Twenty-four hours filled with amazing sex, interrupted only by food and talk.

Time to get to work. But Livvy was snuggled into him. Wrapped around him, really, one leg tucked between his, her breasts flattened against his back. Her hand was wedged between his arm and his chest, and a thick curl of her hair trailed over his shoulder. It tickled his nose when he turned to glance at her.

Easing away from her slowly so he didn't wake her, he rolled over and drew her against his chest. She murmured in her sleep and squirmed closer. Her hair still smelled like oranges, and he inhaled deeply as he stroked his hand down her back.

He was...content. Happier than he could remember being in a very long time. He wanted to lie here and watch Livvy sleep for the rest of the morning.

Unfortunately, twenty-four hours in bed was already too many. He had a job to do, and so did Livvy.

He slid away from her, swallowing at her unhappy murmur. Turning to drag the blanket over her, he saw the purple bruises stretching down her left arm and left leg.

Souvenirs of her close call at Daley Plaza. Bates' fault.

Anger churned in his gut as he got out of bed, threw on his clothes and strode into Livvy's kitchen. He'd talk to Anson today. See if he could get any information out of him. It wouldn't be easy – Bates wasn't a trusting kind of guy. But Ryan had to end this charade. Find the information that would stop Bates' attempt to get bail before Livvy got hurt again.

Yanking open her refrigerator, he shoved aside the leftover pizza from the night before and spotted a carton of eggs. An opened package of English muffins – three left. Opening the freezer, he found the holy grail.

Bacon.

God was looking out for him. He'd fallen in lo...found the only woman in Chicago who had bacon in her freezer.

Depositing his finds on the counter, he started coffee brewing, then found pans to cook the bacon and the eggs.

Fifteen minutes later, he carried a cup of coffee into the bedroom and sat down on the bed. "Hey, sleepyhead," he said, waving the coffee under her nose. "Time to get up."

Livvy cracked one eye open and spotted the mug. "Is that coffee?" she said, struggling upright.

"It is. Breakfast is almost ready." He handed her the mug and swept his gaze over her naked body, his cock stirring. "Join me in the kitchen. Clothing optional."

She grinned at him over the rim of her cup, and he wanted to lean over and kiss her. Slide into bed and pick up where they'd left off last night. Instead, he walked back to the kitchen. Food. Then work. They'd be out the door in half an hour. They could play later.

An hour later, after breakfast and a very long shower, Livvy nipped at his ear as they threw their clothes on. "Sorry

I distracted and delayed you," she murmured, leaning against him as she pulled on a pair of boots. "I don't know what I was thinking."

"I have a pretty good idea," he said, nuzzling her hair as he wrapped an arm around her waist to steady her. "Because I was thinking the same thing."

He'd completely lost track of time. All he'd been thinking about was Livvy.

It was scary as hell.

"Great minds," she said, glancing up at him, and he had to stop himself from leaning in to kiss her again.

He stepped away as soon as her boots were on, and she looked around and grabbed her briefcase. Stilled.

"Ready to go?" He followed her gaze to the briefcase. Saw its smears of mud from its slide across Daley Plaza after the accident. "Let me clean that off."

He hurried into the kitchen, his anger bubbling beneath the surface. Fucking Anson.

Five minutes later, the briefcase clean, he handed it back to her. "You sure you want to go to work today?" he asked.

"Absolutely. I'm a little sore, but otherwise fine."

He opened the back door, scanned the yard and the alley, then rested his hand on his gun as they descended into the back yard. Livvy unlocked the garage, and they got into his car. She'd given him the key yesterday and suggested he park in the garage to get his car off the street.

As he slid into the driver's seat of the SUV, he nodded at the tarp-covered car next to him. "What's that?"

"That's Betsy. Cilla's car. She keeps it in the garage here."

"Yeah, you mentioned Betsy a couple of days ago."

"Vintage Mustang. She and our dad rebuilt it."

"Yeah? You weren't kidding when you said she was a gearhead." Any other time, he'd whip off that tarp and check out the Mustang. Instead, he slid into the car. He needed to focus on business.

Livvy pressed the garage door opener he'd grabbed from

her car when he'd moved it to the street, and he backed into the alley.

"You need to stay in your office today," he said, once they were on Lake Shore Drive and heading toward the Loop. "Don't leave your building. Understand?"

"I'm supposed to have lunch with one of the other state's attorneys," she said, frowning. "We have a case going to trial in two weeks, and we have to go over some final details."

"Can you postpone it for a day?"

"No. This is his last chance to get together. He's starting another trial tomorrow."

Ryan drummed his fingers on the steering wheel. He didn't like this. "You know the guy?"

"Yes. I've worked with him on a couple of other trials."

"Why can't you stay in the building and meet in your office or his?"

"His office is in a different building. We meet at the restaurant across the street from the Daley Center. He's always late and never has enough time for the security line."

"He sounds like a pain in the ass."

She shrugged one shoulder. "He is, but we don't get to choose who we work with." She leaned over and kissed his cheek as she squeezed his thigh. "Sometimes, though, that works out pretty well."

He turned his head to capture her mouth before the light turned green, pulling away only when the car behind his honked. "You're right," he said, pushing on the accelerator. "I owe that bastard Swenson."

He glanced at her as they got closer to her building. "I'm not happy about that meeting. But if there's no other way, make sure you're in the middle of a big group of people before you leave the building. And when you cross the street."

"I'll call Cilla and have her walk me across the street. She was pissed off yesterday morning because I didn't let her stay. She'll be thrilled to have something to do. Okay?"

"Yeah. That would be good."

He rolled to a stop in front of her building, threw on the gumball, and left the car at the curb as he walked her inside. As she turned to get on an elevator, he grabbed her hand. "Be really careful, Livvy. Please."

She twined her fingers with his and squeezed. "Believe me, I will. It'll be fine, Ryan. The restaurant is full of lawyers. Cops, too. It's probably the safest place I could be, besides my office."

He wanted to lean in and kiss her. Instead, he rubbed his thumb along the back of her hand. "I'll see you this afternoon. Wait in the lobby for me."

"Okay." She smiled up at him, and his damn heart fluttered. "See you tonight."

He watched her as she headed for the elevator. Got in, still smiling, and waved as the door closed.

This was supposed to be fun. No strings attached. Nothing but surface intimacy.

He was in trouble.

CHAPTER THIRTEEN

Ryan sat in his car at 28th and California, staring at the massive grey stone building's barred windows. His gaze swept over the forbidding walls topped with razor wire. The armed men in towers at the corners.

Cook County Jail. Home to almost nine thousand men and women, including his former partner, Anson Bates.

The guy who'd hired the most expensive defense attorney in Chicago to get him out on bail. Right before Livvy Marini had almost been run down in a brazen attack in the Daley Center plaza.

Ward curled his fingers around the steering wheel until his knuckles whitened. He stared at his hands as fury burned through him like wildfire

He closed his eyes and thought of Livvy instead – her smile. The way she nestled into him, as if nothing else in the world mattered. The way she'd waved at him as the elevator door closed this morning.

His rage dissipated, and he released his grip on the steering wheel. Flexed his cramping fingers.

He had to let go of his anger. Swallow this hatred for

Anson. Going into that building with his fists clenched and his heart slamming against his ribs would get him nowhere.

Anson would laugh at him. Taunt him. Refuse to give up a single drop of information.

As much as it sickened him, he had to make Anson believe Ryan was on his partner's side. That he wanted to help.

Ryan breathed in and out until his heart rate was steady. Until the top of his head didn't feel as if it was about to blow off. Taking one final deep breath, he avoided thinking about Livvy. About what Anson had done.

He remembered only the man he'd idolized, the man who'd been a father figure to him. The guy who'd taken Ryan under his wing and taught him how to be a cop.

But what kind of cop had Anson taught him to be? The kind who roughed a suspect who'd accused Ryan's partner of stealing from her?

Apparently, Ryan had substituted one lousy father for another one.

Ryan slammed the car door behind him and strode toward the jail's front door. As he stepped inside, the overwhelming prison smell hit him like a fist. Industrial-strength cleaners. Thousands of men and women who showered only twice a week.

Rage. Despair.

Swallowing hard, he gripped the counter at the visitor's window. "Ryan Ward to see Anson Bates."

He slid his badge and identification beneath the bulletproof glass. Signed the log with his name, the time and who he was visiting. Scanned the page, looking for anyone who'd visited Bates earlier that day. No one.

Twenty minutes later, he sat in a small carrel and watched the door open. Bates sauntered in wearing an orange prison jump suit. His face was sallow and puffy as he slid into the seat on the other side of the glass.

"Ward." Bates' eyes narrowed. "What are you doing here?"

Ryan lifted one shoulder. "Just checking in. How you doing?"

"Hanging in." Bates studied his former partner suspiciously. "Heard you were talking to that jerkoff Swenson."

"Had no choice." Ryan allowed his anger to show, knowing Bates would think it was aimed at Swenson. "It was either talk to the SAs, or end up in here myself on that bogus assault charge." The rough way he'd questioned the woman who'd accused Bates of stealing her drug money would be a stain on his soul forever.

"I'm trying to throw them useless scraps, but it's pissing me off," Ryan continued. He thought of what Bates had done to Livvy and allowed the anger to build. "You may be an asshole, Anson, but you're *my* asshole. My partner. They got nothing useful from me."

Bates relaxed back into his seat. "Knew I could count on you, Ward. I got a new lawyer. He's pretty sure he can get me bail. Those asshats at the state's attorney's office are crapping their pants."

"That would be great, but it's not gonna happen." Not if Ryan had anything to do with it. "Swenson has a hard-on for you. He's not letting you out."

"My new attorney has some juice. Bennett knows the right judges to ask. He knows who's pro-police and who's not."

"It's not just the judge. You still have to get past the state's attorneys." Bates would be suspicious if Ryan wasn't logical. If he didn't speak the obvious truth.

"Don't worry about them. That problem has been taken care of."

A chill shivered down Ryan's back, but he scooted his chair closer to the glass, as if he didn't want to be overheard. "They're pretty cocky. They think they have a solid case against you."

"We'll see, won't we?" Bates smirked at him. "Have a beer with me when I get out? For old times' sake?"

"You got it. We'll get together at the Pipe and Shamrock."

Bates' mouth thinned in sudden anger. "I miss that damn place. Miss a lot of shit."

"Sounds like you won't miss it for much longer."

"Damn straight." Bates put his fist against the glass, and Ward pressed his on the opposite side. It made him sick to act like he was on Bates' side.

"Nothing you need?" Ward asked as he pushed his chair away from the carrel.

"I'm good." Bates studied him through the glass. "You coming again next week?" His old partner's smug confidence that he still controlled Ryan made Ryan want to slam his fist into the plexiglass separating them.

Two months ago, he would have felt bad for Anson. Now he felt nothing.

"If you're not out on bail by then." He rapped on the Formica twice, then stood up. "Next week, man."

He walked away from the visitors' area, through the corridor and out of the building. He dragged in a lungful of fresh air to wash away the taste of prison that coated his mouth and clung to his skin. The bitter residue of pretending to be on Anson's side.

He glanced at his watch. Almost noon. Maybe he could get downtown and walk Livvy to her appointment at the restaurant.

A black Escalade with heavily tinted windows rolled to a stop in the parking lot, and a man got out of the passenger side. He headed for the door without glancing at Ward, but Ryan stilled. He knew that guy.

Didn't know his name, but he'd seen the guy with Bates.

His instincts buzzing, Ryan flipped through his memories, but couldn't identify the man. Couldn't remember where he'd seen him.

He could wait ten minutes and walk back into the building. Check out the sign-in sheet. He glanced at his watch. If he did that, he wouldn't make it back in time to escort Livvy to the restaurant.

Stepping into his car, he glanced at his clock and started his engine. He could call the visitor center on his way downtown. Ask them who'd checked in around 11:48.

Before he put his car into gear, he made sure his Bluetooth was working, then scrolled through his contact list until he found the jail. Pressed connect.

* * *

At ten minutes before noon, Livvy put down her pen and threw on her coat. She shoved her wallet and phone into her briefcase, along with her file on the case she shared with Schmidt, then headed for the elevator. She wasn't a big fan of Cory Schmidt – her fellow ASA was arrogant and always late. On top of that, he was a mansplainer. Fatal flaw, as far as she was concerned.

Still, she had to meet with him and coordinate their strategy for the upcoming trial. It was her case, but he was the second chair and she needed to lay out what she wanted from him.

She had to walk to the restaurant by herself, too. Cilla wouldn't be waiting for her on the first floor. She'd gotten a case and was tied up. Her sister had offered to send someone else, but Livvy told her no. She'd take her chances with a big group, rather than trust someone she didn't know.

Once on the first floor, Livvy waited until a crowd of ten or twelve people began drifting toward the Winking Judge pub. She inserted herself in the middle of the group, exchanging pleasantries with a woman from her office.

As they crossed the street, she whipped her head from side to side, watching every car on the street. No one was speeding. The sidewalk was clear.

She saw nothing out of the ordinary.

Inside the pub, she took a deep breath, releasing the dread that had built with every step she'd taken. She'd made it. She was safe. She could meet with Schmidt, and maybe by the time they were done, Ryan would be finished at the jail. He could walk her back to the building.

The pub was crowded, as it usually was at lunch, but a couple was rising from a booth by the window. Livvy started toward it, then hesitated. She'd be an easy target behind that big pane of glass.

But there were no other tables, and she didn't want to sit at the bar to work. Much easier at a table. So she slid into the booth and looked around for Schmidt.

He wasn't there. The jerk was late. As usual.

Huffing with irritation, she opened her file and glanced at her notes. She started a list of things to ask him. She was almost finished when a man slid into the booth across from her.

She looked up with a professional smile. It slid off her face. Not Cory Schmidt. James Dugger.

The man who'd dated her a couple months ago so he could get hold of her files on one of his friends.

"Dugger. Get out of my booth. I'm waiting for someone."

"Hey," he said, with that smile that had attracted her at first. Now she saw it for the smarmy, phony façade that it really was. God, she'd been an idiot.

"I saw you in the window, so I popped in," he said. "I want to apologize to you."

She stared at him for a moment, unmoved by the regret in his expression. There was a little too much calculation in his eyes.

I'll call you if anything unusual happens.

Remembering her promise to Ryan, she fumbled her phone out of her briefcase. "Hold on a minute, Dugger. I've got a call coming in."

She glanced down at the phone in her lap and pressed Ryan's number.

"Hey," she said, forcing herself to smile. "What's up? I'm talking to a guy I know."

"Liv. What's wrong?" Ryan's voice. Thank God. He

wasn't still in the jail.

"James Dugger. I dated him a while ago, remember? You met him that night at the bar in River North. He saw me through the window at the Winking Judge and popped in."

"On my way."

"Yeah, that's him. Yeah, I'll tell him you said he was cute. Gotta go, Jules. I'll call you back later."

Her hands trembling, she disconnected. Held the phone gripped in her hand. Stared at Dugger, willing him to disappear. When he didn't move, she said, "Okay, you've apologized. Leave. I have work to do."

"I kicked myself for weeks afterward, Liv. You were so great. We were so good together. And I blew it by doing something stupid. For a guy I didn't even really know."

Livvy knew exactly how well Dugger had known David Blaine — Cilla had filled her in on their shared drug dealing business in college. "Fine. You're sorry. You made a mistake. It's over. Leave."

"You have to listen to me, Livvy. I want a fresh start."

"Not going to happen. You're out of your mind if you think it will." She glanced around for Schmidt, but he wasn't here. Half an hour had passed since she'd sat down in the booth. He was usually late, but not this late.

Suddenly uneasy, she stood up to leave. Dugger reached up and grabbed her wrist. Squeezed way too hard.

"Sit back down, Livvy." His smile had disappeared. "So I can tell you how this is going to work."

She tried to yank her hand away from him, but he squeezed more tightly. Pain arced up her arm, as if he were grinding her bones together.

"Sit. Down." He lifted something from his lap, and the light glinted off it.

He had a gun. Pointing at her.

* * *

His hands shaking, Ryan pressed Cilla's number.

"Marini."

"Cilla. Thank God you answered. This is Ward. Who's James Dugger?"

"He's a dirtbag Livvy dated a while ago. Why?" Her voice sharpened.

"Livvy was meeting a guy she worked with at The Winking Judge. Across from her building. Dugger showed up."

"Oh, my God. I'm on my way." Ryan heard her saying something to Sobieski. Footsteps running.

"Tell me," he demanded.

"The dating was a set-up. He wanted to get a look at one of her files. A guy she was prosecuting."

"What was the guy's name?" Ryan asked, reaching for the switch to turn on his lights. He had a really bad feeling about this.

"David Blaine. Drug dealer."

The guy he'd seen at Cook County Jail. Visiting Bates. Ryan turned on his siren as well and stepped on the gas. "Gotta go."

* * *

Frozen in place, Livvy stared down at Dugger.

His face hardened. "People are watching, Liv. Unless you want to die right now, sit down."

"As opposed to what, Dugger? Dying later?"

"As opposed to you and a bunch of other people dying right now. Your choice, Livvy."

He leveled the gun at her chest, his hand rock-steady. How could no one else in the restaurant see this? Wasn't anyone paying attention?

No. Her body shielded the gun from the rest of the people. And everyone was involved in their own conversation. Their lunch.

Her legs wobbling, she slid back onto the seat, frantically

trying to figure out a plan. She could jump up and bolt. Run for the door. It was harder to hit a moving target. That's what all the self-defense classes said.

"I'm sitting. What's this all about?"

"You're going to come with me, Liv. We're going to walk out of this restaurant and get in my car. We're going to have a conversation."

"I have nothing to talk to you about." She swallowed the hard lump in her throat. "I told you, I'm meeting someone here. He should be here any minute. So leave now, while you have a chance."

Dugger smiled. "Schmidt? Don't worry about him. He has his orders. He's not showing up."

Ice cold fear spread through her veins, and she began to shake. "What do you mean, he has his orders?" She was afraid she knew exactly what Dugger meant. But she needed to keep him talking. Stall whatever plan he had. Ryan would get here. He'd be in time.

"Schmidt has a drug problem. He owes a guy a lot of money. He's paying it off."

Livvy swallowed past the terror backing up in her throat. She read thrillers. She knew how this worked. Dugger wouldn't tell her all this unless he was going to kill her.

She had nothing to lose by fighting back. "So you're going to shoot me in here? In front of all these lawyers and cops? You think you'll make it out the door?"

"I'm not an idiot, Livvy. I have a suppressor on the gun. I'll shoot you here if I have to, and no one will notice. Stop stalling. Stand up. We're leaving."

* * *

Panic and anger filled Ryan's chest and shortened his breaths. *Livvy.* He was a block away. He'd switched off his siren two blocks ago. His lights were still flashing, but the intersection was blocked. There was nowhere for the cars in front of him to go.

Fear coiled more and more tightly inside him, until finally he threw open his door and raced down the street, resting his hand on his gun as he ran. When he got close to The Winking Judge, he slowed to a fast walk. As if he were late for a meeting, but not late enough to run.

As he reached the pub, he saw Livvy sitting in a booth at the window. A man sat across from her. Ryan spotted the gun in his hand and drew a shaky breath as he stepped into the pub. Breathed in, then out, before he turned toward Livvy's booth.

He walked past Livvy but didn't look at her. Couldn't. If he saw fear on her face, or panic, he'd lose his focus. Make a mistake.

So he smiled and waved, as if meeting someone in a booth along the wall. As soon as he passed Dugger, he pulled out his gun and put it to the asswipe's head.

"Drop the gun, Dugger. Right now."

Dugger froze.

"I don't see that gun on the table and your hands in the air in two seconds, you're a dead man. One. T.."

The gun clattered onto the table. Dugger raised his hands.

The restaurant went completely silent.

Still holding his gun, Ryan yanked Dugger out of the booth and shoved him to the floor. He slapped on cuffs and dropped his gun back into his holster. Then he hauled Dugger to his feet and patted him down. Wasn't gentle about it, either.

He found a sheathed knife in Dugger's jacket. Six inch blade. Thinking about what Dugger might have done to Livvy with that knife, Ryan's stomach churned.

One hand on Dugger's collar, he dialed 911 with his cell. "This is Detective Ryan Ward. I have a suspect in an attempted murder at The Winking Judge. Across from the Daley Center. I need a patrol car ASAP."

Dugger took a step toward the door, and Ryan yanked him back. "Down on the floor," he snarled. "Now."

Dugger dropped to his knees. Lowered himself to the floor, face down.

Two uniformed cops elbowed their way through the gawking crowd. "You need a hand?" one of them asked.

"Yeah." Ryan's hands shook as the adrenaline spiked in his veins. "Take him outside. Wagon's on its way. I'll be there in a minute."

The two uniforms each took one of Dugger's arms and hoisted him into the air. Then, holding his arms, they led him out the door.

Finally, Ryan reached for Livvy. She sat in the corner of the booth, her face white, her eyes huge. Dark.

"Liv," he said, drawing her out of the booth. He drew her into his arms. Closed his eyes and inhaled her scent. "Liv."

She wrapped her arms around his waist and gripped him tightly. She shook violently, her tears soaking his shirt.

"Oh, god, Ry. I was so scared."

"I know, babe." He smoothed one hand down her back. "I know."

She sniffled against his shirt and gripped his waist. She'd leave bruises, and he'd cherish every one of them. They meant she was alive.

"I knew you'd come," she said. "I knew you'd get here in time."

CHAPTER FOURTEEN

Ryan stood in The Winking Judge, his arms tight around Livvy. He ignored the people crowding close. The questions thrown at them from every direction. The wailing siren announcing the arrival of a squad car.

Instead, he breathed in her sweet orange scent. Felt her toned muscles beneath his hands, her now-familiar shape molded against him. The tickle where strands of her hair caught in his scruff. All proof Livvy was alive. That Dugger hadn't hurt her.

Nothing else mattered.

"Livvy!" Cilla's voice.

Livvy lifted her head from his neck and stepped away. She reached for his hand, though, twining her fingers with his and clutching as if she never wanted to let go. "Cilla. How did you…?"

Her sister jerked her head at him. "Ward called me. Asked me about Dugger. Said you'd called." She grabbed Livvy and squeezed hard, knocking Ryan's hand out of the way. "You were so damn smart to call him like that."

Cilla finally let Livvy go. Cilla turned to Ryan and threw

her arms around him. "You got here in time. Thank God."

Wetness seeped into Ryan's shirt as he awkwardly patted Cilla's back. Was Cilla Marini *crying* on him? The tough woman who could stare down any vicious, hard-assed perp?

The cold-as-stone woman who'd arrested him?

"Yeah," he said as Cilla's shoulders shook beneath his hand. "Afraid I was gonna have to put on the Bat Suit and grab the Bat Car. Would have blown my cover."

Cilla hiccupped a laugh and pushed him away. "Too bad, Bat Boy." She sniffled. "I bet Livvy would love to see you in that skin-tight suit."

Cilla took a deep breath, then turned to the crowd surrounding them. Pulling her badge off her belt, she held it up. "Everyone back off. Sit down until we can get people in here to take your statements. We see anyone on their phone? It'll be confiscated." She glanced up to see two more squad cars pull up. "We clear?" She glanced around the room before she nodded once and headed outside.

Ryan curled his arm around Livvy's shoulder and steered her out the door. Three squads now had the street blocked off in front of the pub. Dugger was gone – the first squad car had whisked him away.

Ryan kept his arm around Livvy as she told the uniforms what had happened. Then he said, "There are a bunch of witnesses in there. We need statements from all of them. Detective Marini already warned them about cell phone use."

He took a deep breath as the cops headed into the pub. The air in the pub stunk of spilled beer and fear. Out here, it smelled like the Loop – exhaust and burnt toast. "Let's get out of here. Want to go home?"

Livvy shook her head, not letting go of him. "I want to tell Gus what happened, then give my statement. I want to make sure Dugger doesn't wiggle out of this."

"You sure you don't want to go home?" He drew her closer. "You can give your statement tomorrow."

"No," she said, her voice fierce. "I don't want to forget

a single detail. He was going to drag me to his car, take me somewhere and kill me. I refused to leave. If you hadn't arrived when you did, he would have shot me in that booth."

A fresh wave of rage swept over him. His hands itched to get hold of Dugger. He wanted to rip the dirtbag apart, one limb at a time. He could almost feel his hands around the bastard's throat, squeezing the life out of him.

He'd threatened Livvy. Scared her. Came close to killing her.

If Dugger had hurt her, or worse, killed her, Ryan would have been wrecked. Completely destroyed. He never would have gotten over Livvy.

Whoa! A wild rush of panic swirled through him. That's not what he meant. What happened to fun? Uncomplicated? He wasn't supposed to think his life would be over if he lost Livvy.

He'd promised himself this wasn't a long-term thing with her.

It was the heat of the moment, he told himself. The adrenaline rush and the fury Dugger had released in him. His emotions were all over the map. Things would go back to normal after the burn subsided. He'd be able to think straight again.

He glanced at Livvy as he guided her across the street, still holding her tight against his side. They'd get back to what they'd been before this – hanging out, talking, great sex.

She didn't wait for him to open the door to the Daley building. Before he could grab the handle, she yanked the door open and walked in, ramrod straight. Determined. Unwavering. The strongest woman he'd ever known.

The truth hit him squarely between the eyes – there was no going back to not-serious with Livvy Marini. He was already too far gone. Already in lo… Panic bubbled up like a geyser again.

He wasn't ready for this. Not for a real relationship, the kind that involved commitments. Promises. The white picket fence and two point four children.

He had no idea how relationships worked. No idea how to share his life with a partner. He'd end up hurting Livvy, and that was the last thing he wanted.

What the hell was he going to do?

* * *

Long hours later, Ryan watched two uniforms haul Dugger out of the interrogation room and off to holding. The detective who'd questioned him stood at the door, watching Dugger go, his signed confession in her hand. James Dugger would be shipped off to Cook County tomorrow to await a bond hearing.

Ryan would do his best to make sure it was denied.

Livvy was slumped against him, sound asleep, her head resting in the crook of his arm. His limb had gone numb an hour ago, but he hadn't wanted to wake her.

He could sit here for hours, watching her sleep.

Watching the steady rise and fall of her chest, knowing she was alive.

They couldn't sit in the observation room all night, though. She'd have a sore neck and his arm would fall off. "Hey, Liv," he murmured, kissing her head. "Wake up, babe."

Her eyes fluttered open, and she smiled up at him, open and happy. Because she was with him.

It felt as if she'd punched him in the gut.

She shifted to look at the observation room and frowned. "Where did he go?"

"On his way to Cook County. Julia Carlton got a confession out of him. We've already rounded up David Blaine, and once Blaine found out Dugger was talking, the detective interrogating him couldn't get Blaine to shut up.

"He got an expensive lawyer, and the slick son of a bitch got Blaine and Dugger both a deal. They're not going to get as much time as they deserve. If it were up to me, they'd go away for life. But they've implicated Bates in a lot of crimes. Anson's not getting bail. He's not going anywhere for a long time. I'm guessing Anson's fancy lawyer has already dumped him."

"What about Cory Schmidt?"

"Picked him up, too. He's still claiming he was held up in a meeting, but they'll find what they need on him. Especially after what Dugger said about him being on Bates' payroll."

He smoothed a hand down her hair. "Not much more we can do here. Do you want to go home?"

"Yes," she sighed, laying her head on his shoulder. "Take me home, Ryan."

* * *

Livvy watched the streetlights flickering past as Ryan drove north on Lake Shore Drive. He hadn't said much since they got in the car. He'd asked if she was hungry. Cold. Asked if she wanted to tilt her seat back so she could sleep. Otherwise, he'd been silent.

As he turned onto her street, she swiveled to face him. "You can put your car back in the garage. I'm leaving my car on the street tonight. It'd be silly to waste the parking space."

"That's okay," he said, slowing at a smallish parking spot two buildings down from hers. "This is fine."

He slid the car into the spot with the ease of a seasoned Chicago driver, then plucked her garage door opener from his visor. "Stash this in your briefcase to remind yourself to put it back in your car."

"Isn't that your job?" she teased, reaching for the door handle. "Reminding me to do things to keep myself safe?"

He stared down at his hands. "I'm not sure you need me for that. You did a pretty good job keeping yourself safe today."

"I'll always need you, Ryan." She reached for his hand

and twined her fingers with his, squeezing hard. His hand was stiff and cold, but he eventually squeezed back. Then he let her go as he climbed out of the car.

Livvy stepped into the cold night air, watching Ryan come around the car. He was still avoiding her gaze.

She began to shiver. The cold had seeped beneath her skin and burrowed into every corner of her body. Her ice-filled chest made it hard to breath.

Something was wrong.

"Ryan? Are you okay?"

Maybe it was a delayed reaction to everything that had happened today. He'd told her about his visit with Anson. He'd rescued her from Dugger. They'd both given statements, and they'd watched hours of interrogations.

Maybe he was just exhausted.

"Let's go inside, Livvy," he said.

Or maybe it wasn't just fatigue or the aftermath of an adrenaline rush.

Her heart racing, her stomach twisting with nerves, she fumbled with the key to unlock the front door. Walked up the stairs slowly, every muscle and joint stiff with anxiety. Finally, once they were in her apartment, she turned on the lights and turned to him.

"Something's wrong, Ryan. What is it?"

He rubbed a hand over his face. "What makes you think that?"

"You've hardly said two words to me since we left the First District station. You won't even look me in the eye."

He met her gaze then. "What do you want from me, Livvy?"

Everything. She wanted the whole nine yards with Ryan. "I'm exhausted, and I'm sure you are, too. Why don't we just go to bed? Remind each other that we're both still alive. We can worry about the case and the loose ends in the morning."

"I shouldn't stay, Livvy. I don't belong here."

"What are you talking about? This is exactly where you

belong." She reached for him, but he eased away from her.

He scrubbed his hands across his face. "I can't be with you, Livvy. I'm a mess. A lousy cop, a lousy brother, a lousy son. I can't give you what you need. What you deserve. What I want you to have."

"The man I've gotten to know this past week isn't a lousy cop. You've fought as hard as anyone could to keep Bates in jail. And there's no way I believe you could be a lousy brother or son."

"We've spent a lot of time together, but you don't really know me, Livvy. If you did, you'd run as fast as you could." He took a step back from her. Closer to the door.

"That's not true, Ryan." She wrapped her arms around her waist, trying to brace herself against the shaking. "I care about you, Ryan. I'm looking forward to seeing what normal life is like with you."

"Are you sure, Liv? Because maybe all we had was forced closeness because of the case. Maybe I was just a port in the storm because you were scared."

All we *had*.

She swallowed around the huge lump in her throat. "Not for me. I..." She swallowed again. Maybe it was too soon, but she knew how she felt. She stepped closer to him. "I love you, Ryan. Which is odd, right now, because you're being a real ass. But I do. You're not a port in the storm," she added, biting the inside of her cheek to stop the tears that wanted to fall. "Not 'forced closeness'. I love you."

He edged toward the door. Put one hand on the doorknob. From five feet away, she saw his knuckles whiten. "I'm...I really like you, Liv. You mean a lot to me. But I can't jump into a relationship with you. I'm screwed up. I wish I was worthy of you, but I'm not."

"I thought we were already in a relationship," she said, struggling to keep her voice level.

"I thought this was a 'have fun while we can' kind of thing. Easy. Great while it lasted. No strings attached."

Her eyes prickled, and she drew herself up. She would

not cry in front of him. "I know that's your usual thing. But I thought we had more than that."

"I'm not relationship material." He twisted the doorknob, as if desperate to escape. From her. "I have to get my head on straight before I can get involved with anyone else."

"You don't have to change for me. I love you the way you are."

"I have to change for *me,* Livvy." He yanked the door open. Slid one foot over the threshold.

Her lip trembled, and she bit down on it. Maybe he'd always had one foot out the door, and she'd just been too besotted to see it.

"I have to go, Liv. I can't...I can't be with you."

"So this is one of those 'it's not you, it's me' things?"

"Yes."

"I don't think so." Finally, anger blurred the edges of the pain. "I think you're a coward who doesn't want to commit. Thanks for the help keeping Bates in jail. Now go to hell."

She shoved him all the way out the door and slammed it behind him. He didn't leave – she'd have heard the stairs squeaking. For a long moment, she imagined she heard him breathing on the other side of the wood.

Finally, he headed down to the vestibule. When the door closed behind him, she sank to the floor, put her head on her knees and wept.

* * *

Empty and numb, Ryan sat in his parked car for a long time, staring up at Livvy's apartment. Light bled out the windows at the edges of the blinds, creating an aura of brightness around her apartment. A sign of life.

Was Livvy crying behind those blinds? He'd seen her eyes filling. Seen her bite her lip to stop the tears from falling.

Or was she angry? Throwing things? Cursing him?

He hoped she was angry. He didn't want to think about her crying, devastated by his betrayal. The agony of that picture made him want to run upstairs and tell her he didn't mean it. That he wanted to stay with her.

He forced himself to start his car and pull away from the curb. He drove past her building without looking up again.

He didn't know how a real relationship worked. His own broken family was a piss poor example, and it was the only one he had. He didn't want to wreck Livvy. She mattered too much.

So instead, he'd wrecked them proactively.

His heart told him to go back. Hold her. Celebrate life with her, and try to figure out a way together.

Instead, he pressed down on the accelerator and kept driving.

She might not see it right now, but he was doing what was best for Livvy.

Even though it left him completely hollowed out inside.

The next morning, after staring at the ceiling all night, he picked up his phone. His hand hovered over the keyboard for several minutes. Finally he punched in the numbers and made an appointment with Mary, the department therapist he'd seen after Cilla arrested him.

He didn't like himself very much right now. He needed help to figure out how to fix that.

CHAPTER FIFTEEN

Six weeks later

Ryan pulled into a visitor's parking spot at an apartment complex in the Chicago suburb of Bloomingdale. The formerly white paint on the half-timbered buildings was grey and peeling. Several cars rested on blocks in the residents' parking spots. Garbage overflowed a rusting green dumpster.

Cammie lived in this dump.

He'd found his sister through a police report. She'd been arrested in the nearby suburb of Glendale Heights for disturbing the peace and drunk and disorderly. The arresting officer had found a bag of weed in her purse that barely squeaked below the 'intent to deliver' weight.

She'd spent ninety days in jail. According to her parole officer, this depressing, bleak apartment building was her most recent address.

Ryan hadn't been able to find his brother Jesse, and a cold stone had taken up permanent residence in his gut. Scenarios that explained Jesse's absence unspooled constantly in Ryan's brain, each one worse than the last.

After staring at the crooked numbers on the building for too long, working up his courage, he stepped out of the car. Opened the door to the building and walked into the hall.

No inside security door. Decent lighting, but it only highlighted the worn, dirty carpet and the loose railing up to the second floor. His eyes burned at the pungent smell of an industrial strength cleaner that didn't quite cover the stink of vomit.

Cammie's apartment was on the second floor. He stood in front of her door for a long time before he knocked. His heart pounded as he listened for footsteps.

He hadn't seen Cammie since their mother's funeral, five years earlier. Then, Cammie had been a sullen, resentful, eighteen-year-old who had never forgiven him for walking away from their family after his father died when she was eleven.

Five years ago, Ryan had been a newly-minted detective whose partner Anson Bates had drawn him into the cop family. Not blood, but just as close. Finding his place had helped Ryan bury the pain of losing his real family.

Five years ago, his mother's funeral hadn't seemed like the time to tell Cammie and their brother Jesse that his mother had thrown Ryan out of the house after their father died.

The therapist he'd been seeing three times a week had helped Ryan see how he'd made so many bad decisions over the past fourteen years. Chosen the wrong fork in the road more often than not.

She'd also helped him see that he'd made those decisions while floundering in a swamp of family secrets, guilt and loneliness. That he'd been squeezed into a box without the keys to unlock it.

She was helping him dissolve the sticky web of self-reproach and remorse that bound him so tightly to the past. Bonds that he needed to break free of to step into the future.

For the first time in years, he could see daylight through

the trees. It shimmered in front of him, still out of reach, but beckoning him closer. Mary was helping him hack through the brambles that blocked his way. She'd shown him that connecting with Cammie and Jesse again was the next step in the process.

Yeah, he was doing better.

But would it make a difference if Cammie refused to see him? Refused to talk to him?

He knocked again, his foot jiggling on the carpet. Finally he heard footsteps on the other side of the door. His heart banging against his chest, his lungs tight, he swallowed hard as the door opened.

He didn't recognize the woman on the other side of the door. If it was Cammie, she'd dyed her blond hair black. Straightened it. Gained some weight.

"Cammie?" he asked cautiously.

"No. I'm her roommate."

"Is she home?" Ryan stood taller beneath the young woman's assessing gaze.

"She's not here," the woman finally said.

"When will she be back?"

The woman's face hardened and her eyes narrowed. "Why do you want to know?"

"I want to see her," Ryan answered, wondering why Cammie's roommate was so hostile. So suspicious. Was his sister in trouble?

"If you're a bill collector, I'm not telling you jack shit," she said, closing the door.

Ryan stuck his foot out to keep the door open. "I'm not a bill collector. I'm her...friend." He couldn't say he was her brother. If Cammie refused to see him and disappeared, he'd have to start over from scratch.

The woman studied him. Ryan stared back. "Hold on," she finally said. "I'll take a look at her schedule." She kicked his foot away from the door and slammed it shut.

Ryan closed his eyes and took a deep breath. Cammie's roommate wasn't going to look at his sister's schedule. She wouldn't open that door again.

He wasn't about to leave. If Cammie lived here, and apparently she did, she'd come home sooner or later.

Leaning against the wall next to the door, Ryan stared at the crooked letters 'Apt. B' glued to the wood. What had happened to his mother's house? Why wasn't Cammie living there?

Footsteps echoed behind the door. Coming closer. Maybe the roommate was coming back after all.

The door opened and his sister stood in front of him. Her blond hair was cut short and her face was pale and make-up free. Her gray eyes, so similar to his, stared at him, shocked.

"Ryan?" she whispered.

Without waiting for him to answer, she launched herself into his arms. Hugged him tight, her arms a vise around his neck. "Ry," she sobbed into his chest. "My God. You're here."

Ryan closed his eyes and held onto his sister, blinking back his own tears. She felt thin. Fragile in his arms. "Cammie. Oh, God, Cam. I'm so glad I found you."

"How *did* you find me?" She leaned back to look at his face, wiping away tears on the sleeve of her tee shirt. Its stormy gray was the exact color of her eyes.

He knuckled away a tear she'd missed. "I'm a cop, Cam. It's what I do." She didn't ask the question that hung between them – then why didn't you find me earlier?

"Come in," his sister said, throwing the door wide and catching his hand, as if he might run if she didn't hold on.

Ryan stepped into the apartment, but resisted his sister's effort to pull him farther inside. "Do you want to go somewhere we can talk? A restaurant? Or a coffee shop?"

"We can talk here. Jenny's getting ready for work. She's leaving in a few minutes." Cammie grabbed his hand again and tugged him into a small galley kitchen.

It was immaculate. The counters held only a toaster and a battered toaster oven. The sink was free of dirty dishes, and the drying rack was empty.

"You want something to drink?" Cammie asked, opening the refrigerator. "I have iced tea or that flavored fizzy water. Not the expensive brand. But I think it's just as good."

"Iced tea sounds great," he said, scanning the shelves of the refrigerator and seeing only lunchmeat, bread, fruit, bags of salad, butter and condiments. No beer or wine.

She must have seen him looking. "No booze, if that's what you're looking for. I go to AA four times a week," she said quietly. "So does Jenny."

"Do people in AA...are they supposed to live together?"

"Maybe not, but Jenny and I help each other stay sober." She glanced toward the back of the apartment, where he assumed Jenny was. "We lean on each other. It's working for both of us."

"That's good," Ryan said, exhaling. "And for the record, I wasn't looking for booze. I wanted to make sure you had stuff to eat in there."

Cammie pulled a pitcher of iced tea out of the fridge and closed the door. "I'm twenty-three, Ry. I've made mistakes, but I'm learning. Only good food, fizzy water and iced tea in my fridge." She poured two glasses and handed him one. "Let's sit in the living room."

That room was immaculate, as well. The upholstery on the couch and two chairs was worn and faded. The tables looked like they'd been scavenged from someone's curb, but they were clean, too. A few pictures hung on the wall, mostly beach scenes. Cammie had always loved the beach. A small bookcase held a collection of paperbacks.

"You've got a nice place, Cam," Ryan said as he lowered himself onto the couch.

"Thanks." She sat in the chair across from him and set her glass on one of the coasters on the coffee table. "I've learned that if you take care of your place, you're taking care of yourself. Jenny and I have a list of chores and we do them regularly."

He remembered Cammie's room in their family's house. He would have been hard-pressed to name the color of her rug. It had been covered with clothes and papers and books for as long as he could remember.

"How've you been, Cam?"

She studied him for a long moment, then smiled. "I'm doing good, Ry. I have a job. I have friends – the right kind of friends. And I've got a place of my own."

"Where do you work?"

"At the Whole Foods a mile away. I've been there for eight months. I even got a raise."

"That's great, Cam."

"It's not a fancy job," she said. "But I like it, and I'm saving some money. I enrolled in the junior college, and I'm taking an English class. Can't afford more than one a semester, but I'm working my way through the prerequisites."

"For...?"

She rolled her shoulders and avoided his gaze. "I want to be a counselor. In a program for drug addicted teens."

Ryan reached across the table and took his sister's hand. "I'm so proud of you, Cam. You'd be great at that."

"Because I've been there?" she said, raising her chin.

"Yeah, that's part of it." He wasn't going to lie to his sister. "But mostly because you've always been easy to talk to. Beneath the attitude, you were always kind. Caring. Sweet."

He saved all of his overtime pay, and he had a little nest egg. Maybe he could help Cammie take more than one class a semester.

Her lower lip trembled, and she stared down at her lap. "Hearing you say that means a lot to me, Ry."

"It's the truth."

She finally looked up at him. "Looks like you're doing pretty well, too. I saw you on television right after Mom died. You'd solved some case. Everyone seemed pretty happy about it."

He studied his sister. "If you saw me on TV after Mom died, why didn't you come find me?"

She pleated the fabric of her tee shirt, a nervous habit she'd had since she was a kid. "I was an immature jerk, Ry. I blamed you for the way our family disintegrated. The way Jesse took off and never came back, the way Mom was, how screwed up I got."

Ryan swallowed the lump of guilt and sadness swelling in his throat. "I'm sorry, Cam. I let you down. Jesse and Mom, too. I abandoned all of you after Dad died. I wish I could go back and change it, but I can't."

Cammie rolled her eyes. "You didn't abandon us, you idiot. Mom threw you out because she blamed you for getting Dad killed. I might have only been eleven, but I knew what was going on."

Ryan swallowed again, his mouth suddenly dry as dust. "Did she...do you think she ever regretted it?"

"I don't know. Maybe. I heard her in your room once in a while, crying. Not sure if it was because she missed you, though, or missed having someone to help around the house. Doesn't matter. You know how Mom was – she wouldn't ever admit to making a mistake. Wouldn't ever apologize for anything she did."

"I called her a few times," Ryan said, taking a gulp of the unsweetened tea. "She always hung up on me."

"Don't blame yourself, Ry." His sister reached for his hand, and he closed his fingers around hers. "You could have called her every day and she would have hung up on you every time. You called the cops when Dad was knocking her around. The cops threw him in jail. Another inmate shanked him. In her mind, you were the cause of all her problems."

"Yeah. No one could ever tell Mom anything," he said quietly. He'd always wonder if he should have been more persistent. Tried harder. But in his heart, he knew Cammie was right. It wasn't in his mother's nature to forgive.

"I've talked to my therapist about Mom," Cammie said,

fingers tight in her shirt. "Teddy said Mom should never have had kids. That she didn't protect any of us. To throw you out of the house..." She shook her head. "She was always about herself. Not her kids. I think Teddy's right. It's not on you. It's on Mom."

"Still, I should have been able to do *something* for you and Jesse."

Cammie snorted. "I'm guessing you have to deal with a lot of stubborn, screwed-up teenagers." She waited until he nodded once. "Any of them ever listen to you?"

Of course they didn't. He hadn't listened to anyone at that age, either.

"I rest my case. Nothing that happened was on you, Ry. It all started when you called the cops on Dad. And that was the right thing to do," his sister said fiercely.

"Maybe you're right." She was definitely right, but it would take him a while to forgive himself for the way he'd let Cammie and Jesse down.

"I know I'm right," Cammie said. "And speaking of being right..." Cammie leaned forward, smiling.

"I saw you a couple of months ago, too," she said. "About that case with the crooked cop. That woman you rescued from the restaurant? You had your arm around her like you weren't ever gonna let her go." She leaned forward and her hand tightened on his. "I predict I'm getting a sister-in-law sometime soon."

Even now, six weeks later, any mention of Livvy made his chest ache. Cammie's question about Livvy was an arrow straight to the heart. He worked his hand out of his sister's grasp.

"I don't know, Cam. I screwed up. Really badly."

"Didn't seem that way," she said, frowning. "Looked like you were the hero."

"Maybe at the very end. But the whole mess with Bates wasn't my finest hour."

"Your partner was the crook. Not you. So it wasn't your fault."

"So my therapist keeps telling me."

"You're seeing a therapist, too?" his sister said, surprised.

"Yeah." Ryan shrugged, still uncomfortable telling people about Mary. "Is your therapist helping you?"

"Yeah," she said, relaxing back into the chair. "He is. How about you?"

"Mary's great. I'm figuring out a lot of stuff." Whether Livvy would ever be able to forgive him was another story.

Maybe she'd moved on already. Put him out of her head and her life.

Shoving the thought out of his head, he forced a smile. "Hey, Cam, it's almost six. Want to get some dinner?"

She studied him for a long moment, then smiled back. "I'd love that, Ry. We have a lot of catching up to do."

CHAPTER SIXTEEN

Two months later

Ryan sat in the big, comfortable armchair across from Mary, watching his therapist scribble something on a pad of paper. Then she looked up at him. Smiled.

"How are you doing today, Ryan?"

"I'm good. Cammie and I chased down a few leads on our brother Jesse, but they were all dead ends. We're not giving up, though."

"So your relationship with your sister is going well?"

"It's great." He relaxed his grip on the arms of the chair. These were the easy questions. "She signed up for three courses at her junior college this semester. She's going to be busy, but we're still getting together once a week."

"Have you asked her about moving closer to you?"

"Yeah, but she doesn't want to do it. She's happy where she is. She and Jenny have friends, jobs, a routine. Jenny's starting classes at the junior college, too."

"How does that make you feel?"

Ryan remembered his sister's face when they'd had

160

dinner the previous week. She'd glowed when she told him about the three classes she was enrolled in. "It makes me feel good. Really good."

"Are you ready to work on other relationships in your life?"

His stomach clenched. Back to the hard questions. He knew what Mary was asking, and he didn't want to think about Livvy. It had been almost four months since he'd walked out of Livvy's life. For all he knew, she'd moved on. Gotten involved with someone else. A woman like Livvy wouldn't be single for long.

Thinking of Livvy with someone else made him feel as if his heart had been torn out of his chest. As if there was nothing but a void where the organ used to be.

"Other relationships? Yeah, we're still looking for Jesse. Won't stop until we find him."

Mary tapped her pen on her pad of paper as she studied him. "That wasn't who I was asking about."

Ryan didn't say a word.

"Tell me again why you left Olivia?"

Ryan rolled his shoulders. He tried to avoid talking about Livvy with Mary. Everything time they did, it ripped the scab off his heart, leaving it bleeding all over again. "I didn't know how to be in a real relationship. I knew I'd mess up. Hurt her. Ruin everything."

"Do you think you know how to be in a relationship now?"

He shrugged, staring at a painting of a vase of peonies on the wall behind Mary. Trying not to think of Livvy. "Does anyone really know?"

Mary smiled. "Right answer, Ryan. Do you miss her?"

"Every minute of every day." If that wasn't hard enough, he dreamed about her every night, too.

"So if you tried to have a relationship with Livvy, it would hurt very much if you didn't make it."

"Yeah," he said, squirming in the chair. "It would." It would kill him.

"How do you think you'll feel if you let her go for good? Don't even try to get her back?"

Ryan stared at his shoes. Didn't answer. If he never saw Livvy again, the hole in his soul would deepen into an abyss. So deep and so wide that he'd never crawl out of it.

He tried to keep his face expressionless. But Mary was a great therapist. She'd seen his truth. She cocked her head. "You have two choices, Ryan. Which are you going to take?"

* * *

The garage door rumbled down behind Livvy, cutting off the alley light. The dim bulb in the garage ceiling illuminated her car just enough that Livvy was able to grab her briefcase and the brown paper bag holding her Chinese takeout.

Her back ached as she climbed out of her car and slammed the door, and she rolled her shoulders to ease the strain. She'd been working way too much lately, hunched over her computer in her office, but she was glad to have the distraction.

Happy to get home late, too tired to do anything but eat dinner and fall into bed.

Too tired to dream.

Her yard was quiet, the grass encrusted with icy snow. It crunched beneath her boots with that hollow sound the snow made when it was really cold. Her landlord had sprinkled sand on the icy mess, but it was still treacherous. Woozy with exhaustion, she stepped carefully to avoid slipping.

The wooden staircase to her kitchen door echoed dully in the frigid night air as she walked upstairs. She'd forgotten to turn on her porch light. Again. But she managed to shove her key into the new lock.

Ryan had told her she needed a better lock on her back door. A week or two after he'd left, she'd purchased a new one. Brendan had insisted on installing it for her.

Her sister and brother-in-law to-be had done a lot of things for her in the past few months. Pressed her to have dinner with them at least once a week. Cilla called almost every day. Both of them went out of their way to draw her into the Donovan family.

Livvy had resisted at first. Brooding and sad, she knew she wasn't good company. But Cilla had pushed, and everyone in Brendan's family had been welcoming. Friendly. Genuinely happy to see her.

She was a regular at their dinners now. When Helen and Jamie came with their newborn twins Liam and Sean and their toddler Charlotte, she played with Charlotte and took turns holding the boys. It made her eyes prickle with unshed tears, but she refused to mope about Ryan and what they might have had. He'd made his choice. She'd get over him.

Eventually.

After dumping her Kung Pao Chicken onto a plate and plunking it into the microwave, she kicked off her heels and walked into her living room, flicking on all the lights. Ever since the incident with Dugger at The Winking Judge, she didn't like shadows. She wanted to see every corner of her rooms.

Heading for her bedroom, she shed her suit and shirt. Two minutes later, the timer on the microwave dinged as she stepped into the kitchen. Her flannel pajamas and tattered old sweatshirt were warm and comforting after the outside cold.

She'd eaten two mouthfuls of food when her doorbell rang. Ten o'clock at night.

It had been a long time since the mess with Bates, but an unexpected visitor late at night still made her stomach clench and her pulse jump. Swallowing a piece of chicken that suddenly felt as big as a tennis ball, she pushed away from the table and hurried into the living room. She eased the blind away from the window and peered at the door. A

163

tall form stood there, his hands in the pockets of his jacket, a red hat covering his head. He shifted from one foot to the other. Either nervous or cold. Maybe both.

As if the man could feel her watching, he looked up. Held her gaze for a long moment.

Ryan.

She clutched the blind tightly, hard enough to bend the thin metal slats. His face looked...thinner. Older. Weary.

As if maybe he'd suffered from their separation as much as she had.

She let the blind drop into place. He didn't get to feel that way. *He* was the one who'd walked away.

Her heart galloped in her chest and her throat tightened. Did she want to see him?

Yes. More than anything.

Was she ready to see him?

Maybe he'd stopped by to tell her that he wanted another chance with her.

Her chest tightened so much she could barely breathe.

Or maybe he'd come over to tell her that he was moving on, and she should, too.

Her finger hovered over the buzzer. *Yes or no.* Take a chance and know for sure? Or ignore the ringing of the doorbell and avoid more pain?

When did you turn into such a ninny?

She pressed the button to unlock the door downstairs, then glanced at her clothes. Sighed. She'd let him up while she was wearing the rattiest stuff she owned.

Closing her eyes, she took a deep breath. She'd never been the kind of woman who worried about what a guy thought of her clothes. Tonight, though, it would be hard to feel strong and in charge while she wore the clothes she saved for when she needed comfort.

She wished she'd left her suit on. Her armor. The thing she hid behind in court.

Ryan hit the first squeaky stair. Halfway up. He wasn't hurrying. Finally he reached her landing. She imagined she heard him breathing on the other side of the door. Eventually, he knocked. When he did, she took a deep breath and swung the door open.

They stared at each other for a long moment. He looked...good. His face was thinner, as if he'd lost weight, but he wasn't clenching his jaw. His eyes were a soft gray instead of stormy. He seemed relaxed. More open than she'd ever seen him. Happy, even.

Her heart stuttered, then began a slow, heavy beat in her chest. He was happy. Was he here to tell her he was moving on? That would be like Ryan. Honorable. Upfront with her.

Butterflies fluttering in her stomach, a huge ball of anxiety swelling in her chest, she swallowed once and stood aside. "Come in," she said, her voice hoarse. Tight.

"Livvy," he said, his gaze devouring her. "How are you?"

"I'm good. You?"

"Me, too. Good, I mean."

God! Could they *be* more terminally trite?

Rolling her eyes at both of them, she headed for the chair. "Have a seat. What are you doing here? Especially at this time of night."

By the time he sat on the couch, across from her, she had her game face on. She watched him politely. Waiting.

Ryan tugged off his hat and ran a hand through his hair. It stood up from the static electricity in her dry apartment, and she curled her fingers into her palms to keep from reaching for him. Smoothing those light brown waves back into place.

"Livvy, I want to apologize for the way I left things between us." He closed his eyes, regret filling his expression. Finally, elbows on his knees, he blinked twice then studied her for a long moment. His eyes darkened as his gaze drifted over her sweatshirt and plaid flannel pants.

Heat speared into her every place his gaze touched. Way too conscious of being naked beneath the baggy clothes, she pressed her thighs together.

She tucked her feet under her legs to keep them from jiggling on the floor. "Nothing to apologize for. You were very clear about what you needed. What you wanted."

What you didn't want.

"I doubt that." He held her gaze steadily. "Since the only thing I was clear on was that I was scared as all hell."

Livvy tilted her head and frowned. "Scared of what? All the bad stuff was over."

"That was the easy stuff. The hard stuff was still there." He swallowed and ran his hand over his stubbled jaw. The whiskers rasped against his palm, the tiny sound surrounding her. Sending more heat spiking through her body.

She'd loved rubbing her face against his, relished the burn of his scruff against her skin.

He sat unmoving. Watching her.

She swallowed. "What hard stuff?" Taking a deep, steadying breath, she slid her feet out from under her. Leaned closer. "What are you talking about, Ryan?"

"You." He swallowed, but still didn't look away. She had to give him credit for that. "How I felt about you. What I wanted with you."

Her heart rolled over. *Wanted. Felt.* Past tense. "What you wanted with me?" she managed to repeat, despair an icy fist to her chest.

"Not *wanted.*" He shook his head hard enough that a strand of hair fell across his forehead. "Want. Still. Always."

The ice began melting, but she jumped to her feet and paced the room behind the couch, unable to look at his face. Afraid of what she'd see. Or wouldn't see. "And what is that?" Her voice wobbled, and she swallowed the greasy fear.

"I want you," he said, swiveling to face her. "A relationship." He closed his eyes. "*No.* No more dancing around. I'm committed, Livvy. To you. I want forever with you."

Forever? Was he saying what she hoped he was saying?

Trying to get the question out, to ask him what he meant, she couldn't force the words past the huge lump in her throat. Ryan rose from the couch and moved in front of her. She swallowed once, again, but the words were still stuck.

Ryan watched. Waited for her to speak. When she didn't, desolation, bleak and lonely, appeared in his expression. He closed his eyes, hiding the despair in their gray depths.

When he opened them again, the despair was twined with understanding. Resignation. "You've moved on. Found someone else. Or just can't forgive me." He shrugged. "I don't blame you. I was a real ass. I should have told you how scared I was. I should have told you all the things I had to fix in myself. Instead, I walked out the door, when I should have asked you to help me deal with all my crap.

"You told me you loved me." He raised his hand, as if reaching for her, then let it drop. "Do you have any idea how much that meant to me? How much I wanted to say it back to you? Instead, I told you I *liked* you. Hell, I like my car. I like my apartment. I like the barista at Della's."

He opened his eyes. Touched her cheek with a trembling hand. "I *love* you, Olivia Marini. Completely. With all my heart. I'm here to beg you to give me another chance."

Her heart came to life again with a jolt. "Say it again," she murmured, her chest expanding. "Please."

"I'm begging you, Livvy. Please forgive me."

"Not that." She grabbed his hand. "The other."

He stood straighter. His shoulders relaxed, the tension draining away. A hint of mischief twinkled in his eyes. "I like my car?"

"Yes, you ass. That." She tried to hold it back, but a smile lit her face. "I've been waiting four months to hear about your deep attachment to your car."

He tightened his grip on her hand, reached for the other one. He was smiling now, too. "I love you, Livvy. So much. Those three words can't possibly express how much I adore you. Want you. It's going to take years to show you. And I promise I'll do that every single day of every one of those years."

"I've missed you so much," she whispered. "I thought about you every day. Wondered what you were doing. *How* you were doing. You're it for me, Ryan. So if you're not completely sure what you want, leave now. Don't break my heart all over again."

He closed his eyes for a long moment, then drew her into his arms. "I hate that I caused you so much pain. I won't ever forgive myself for that. But I *can* promise you that I'm done leaving. I'll never walk away from you again."

He held her gaze for a long moment, and she saw the assurances there. The pledges. He was here. He loved her. He wasn't going anywhere.

"I got help because of you, Livvy. I'm working to straighten myself out. If not for you, I'd still be floundering." He brushed his hand over her cheek, his touch almost reverent. "You saved me, Livvy. As surely as if you'd stepped in front of a bullet for me, you saved my life."

Her eyes burning, she curled her arms around his neck. "Sounds like you saved yourself," she said, melting into him. "You got help dealing with your problems."

"I wouldn't have done it without you. You made me want to be better."

"And are you? Better?"

"Still a work in progress. But I want to do the work with you."

"And I want to be there for you while you do it," she murmured, her fingers tangling in his hair.

He stared down at her for a long moment, his gaze full of love, his mouth curling into an intimate smile. Then he fumbled in his pocket and brought out a small box.

She gasped, her fingers covering her mouth. "Ryan?" Her voice wavered.

"Marry me, Livvy." He got down on one knee. "Please. You're all I want. Now and forever."

"Yes," she whispered, wrapping her arms around his neck. "I love you so much, Ry." She pressed her mouth against his, kissing him with four months worth of pent-up need. Desire.

He deepened the kiss, drawing her close, and something hard dug into her side. When she flinched, he broke the kiss and rested his forehead against hers. "I think we're doing this backwards, Liv." His voice sawed in and out. He wanted her as much as she wanted him. "I'm supposed to put the ring on your finger before we kiss."

He opened the box and took it out. Light bounced off the diamonds that circled the band, flashing a rainbow on the wall.

"It's beautiful," she said, staring at the band as he slid it onto her finger.

"No beginning and no end. Forever." He lifted her hand and kissed the band of diamonds on her finger. "That's what this ring means. I don't know what road our lives will take, but I do know this – we'll face everything together. Side by side. For the rest of our lives."

They stared at each other for a long moment. Exchanging promises. Vows. Assurances. The heat from his body curled around her, drawing her closer to him.

She moved restlessly, brushing against his solid chest, desire suddenly thick and heavy between them. She wanted more. *Needed* more.

"Aren't you forgetting something?" she asked, leaning into him.

"What? What am I forgetting?" He frowned, and she imagined him wracking his brain, trying to figure out what he hadn't said. What else he needed to say.

"You ever hear the words 'sealed with a kiss'?" she murmured against his mouth.

"God, Livvy." His mouth settled on hers, but instead of devouring her, as she wanted him to do, he trailed a string of tiny, sucking kisses across her face. Down her neck. To that spot beneath her ear he'd found the first time they'd made love.

Finally, when her skin felt two times smaller than her body, when heat poured through her veins and ignited every one of her nerves, she grabbed his ears and pulled his mouth to hers. "Kiss me like you mean it, Ryan," she said, her voice catching in her throat. "Like I've wanted you to kiss me since the night you walked out the door."

He pressed his mouth to hers, slid his tongue along the seam, and she opened eagerly to him. As their tongues danced, she jumped up and wrapped her legs around his waist. Started to unbutton his shirt. "I need you, Ryan. So much. Please."

He cupped her rear in both hands, tracing one finger down the crease of her flannel pants. Exactly where she needed it. "Bedroom," she gasped. "Now. Please."

"We need to talk, babe," he said. "I want to tell you where I've been. What I've been doing."

"Not now," she said into his mouth. "Talk later. Kiss now. I want makeup sex. I need to find out if it's as hot as everyone says it is."

He dived back into the kiss. She was so wrapped up in him, in the joy of touching him again after so long, that she barely felt him moving. Until he set her on her bed and began unbuttoning his shirt.

"I really wanted to talk first," he said, dropping his shirt on the floor and unbuttoning his jeans. "But you have a much better idea. You know how much I like to do research." His jeans hit the floor, and he tugged at her flannel pants. Stilled as he dropped them on top of his jeans. "Commando, Livvy? I'm digging this research thing already."

"No more talking," she said, pulling him down on top of her. "Not for a long, long time."

EPILOGUE

Seven months later

Ryan tore his gaze from Livvy and stood with the rest of the guests at Brendan and Cilla's wedding. Watched as the stunning bride walked down the aisle between the rows of chairs in the Garfield Park Conservatory. Orange and pink mums, yellow asters and sedum, red sneezeweed and multi-colored dahlias lined both sides of Horticulture Hall. The flowers, in their palette of fall hues, framed the gorgeous mosaics of the Zellij fountain that was the centerpiece of the room.

Ryan's gaze touched on the magnificent structure briefly, then returned to Cilla. She radiated happiness. Glowed with joy. And the tiny bump beneath her wedding dress made him smile.

Still, his gaze returned to Livvy as if pulled there by a magnet. Livvy was breathtaking. He'd barely been able to keep his hands to himself on the drive to the conservatory. He was pretty sure she hadn't noticed – she'd been too busy worrying about all the details involved in the wedding.

Now, watching her stand straight and tall in front of the fountain, her wavy hair flowing over her shoulders, a bouquet of orange roses and baby's breath clasped in her hands, he ached for her. As if she sensed his gaze, she glanced at him, her mouth softening in a tiny smile.

He wished this was *their* wedding. He wanted to be watching Livvy walk up the aisle toward him. As Cilla passed him, the quiet rustle of her wedding gown made him glance at the beautiful dress.

He didn't care what Livvy wore to their wedding. She could wear a burlap sack and she'd still be gorgeous. Hell, he'd marry her in her pajamas, if that's what she wanted.

He just wanted to do it *soon*.

Cilla's hand fluttered over her abdomen as she handed Livvy her flowers, and Ryan watched with a tiny stab of envy. He wanted that, too. Children with Livvy. Two, maybe three of them, who'd grow up with the other Donovan kids.

He grinned to himself. Jamie was going to have to expand that new kitchen he'd built for Rose to hold all the Donovan babies he suspected would appear in the next several years.

Ryan had hesitated the first time Livvy asked him to come to dinner at Rose's house. That was family time. He didn't want to intrude. And, honestly, after the way he'd disappeared on Livvy, he didn't want to face the Donovan's disapproval.

She'd persuaded him to give it a try, and he was so glad he had. Everyone in the family had welcomed him, even Brendan and Cilla. Livvy's sister and fiancé would've had every right to be cool toward him. No one would have thought it wrong, including Ryan. But they'd told him they'd forgiven him. That they were glad he'd come back to Livvy. Now, seven months later, he felt as if he were part of the Donovan family, too. Even his sister Cammie had come a few times. Their brother Jesse would join them when he got out of rehab.

That was part of the Donovan magic – they welcomed everyone. Whenever someone new showed up, they handed the newcomer a beverage, brought in another chair, and added a plate to the table.

Drew them into the family circle.

Ryan glanced at the beautiful arching glass above them that framed the royal blue night sky. The sweet scent of flowers surrounded them, the earthy aroma of the plants and soil a rich undertone. Garfield Park conservatory was a beautiful place. But he wanted this ceremony to be over. He wanted to reclaim Livvy, curl his arm around her waist, draw her close enough that he could inhale her tangy, citrusy scent.

He'd been to a bunch of weddings, and they were lots of fun. This one was different, though. It was the first one he'd attended with Livvy, and he wanted to share the magic with her. Celebrate their families together. Dream about their own wedding. Figure out how soon they could make it happen.

* * *

Later that evening, as the DJ spun records and people crowded onto the dance floor in the Show House, Ryan tugged Livvy toward the back of the room, where a group of large tropical philodendrons created a green wall of privacy. "What are you doing?" she said, resisting the tug of his hand. "Don't you want to dance?"

"Want to spend a little time with my fiancée," he murmured, curling his arm around her waist. "Now that you're finished with your official duties."

"Not quite finished," she said, sliding her arm around his waist. "Cilla and Brendan are leaving soon."

"Then we'll have to be quick," he said, letting his hand slip down and caress her hip.

Her eyes went dark. Her chest flushed. "What did you have in mind?" she murmured as he drew her behind the philodendrons.

"Hmm. Let me think about that." He backed her into the wall and covered her mouth with his. Desire, hot and urgent, pounded through him. He slid his fingers beneath the silky black material covering her breast. "Great choice in a dress," he murmured, loving the weight of her soft breast in his hand. "I like it a lot."

Livvy sucked in a breath as he trailed one finger over her nipple. "Ry," she moaned, her body liquid and soft against his. Suddenly, as if she'd just realized where they were, she tensed and pushed him away. "What are you doing?"

"If I have to tell you, Liv, I'm doing it wrong. Let me see if I can do better."

Her nipple pebbled beneath his hand, and she surged against him. "We're in public," she said, breathing heavily. "Anyone could see us." She didn't pull away, though.

"They'll see me kissing my fiancée." He tunneled beneath the dress again and circled her nipple. She pressed into his thigh. Her breath caught, making him flex his leg. She gasped again.

"There's a koi pond a couple rooms over," he murmured. "No one in there. You want to go look at the fish?"

"You want the fish to watch us?" she asked, sliding her hands over his ass.

"They might enjoy it. I sure will." He pressed his hard penis against her. "Wouldn't take long." He sucked her lower lip into his mouth. Let it go with a tiny, wet pop. "If you're as turned on as I am."

He pressed into her again, and she moaned into his mouth. "Which I think you are."

The sound of someone clearing his throat behind them made Ryan freeze. Step away from Livvy and turn around, shielding her from whoever stood on the other side of the green barrier.

"Ah, Liv, Cilla's looking for you." Livvy's brother Sam. "She and Brendan are getting ready to leave."

Ryan felt her take a deep, trembling breath behind him, then she stepped out of the shadows. "Thanks, Sammy. Tell her I'll be right there."

"Don't call me Sammy," he brother said with a scowl.

"Sorry. I forgot you're all grown up. Almost." As she stepped past Ryan, she whispered, "We'll go fishing later. I promise."

They both stepped away from the plants, then Ryan and Sam watched Livvy hurry toward her sister.

"How's it going, Sam?" Ryan asked with a sigh. He liked the kid. He did. He'd met Sam a couple of times, when he and Livvy, along with Brendan and Cilla, had driven to Iowa to watch Sam play for the minor league Cubs. Right now, though, he wished the kid was back in Iowa.

"Good," Sam replied, taking a swig of Goose 312 beer as he watched Livvy and Cilla talking. He glanced at Ryan out of the corner of his eye. "You doing right by Livvy? I don't want to have to kick your ass."

"No reason to do that," Ryan answered. He swallowed a laugh as he admired the sway of Livvy's hips in those killer heels. The kid had bravado, Ryan would give him that, but Sam was a guppie in a shark tank. "Livvy's the best thing that's ever happened to me. I make sure she knows that every single day."

Sam smirked over the neck of his beer bottle. "Judging by the way you two were so...busy behind those plants, I'm guessing she's happy."

Ryan closed his eyes and took several deep breaths. When he was sure he could walk without embarrassing himself, he headed toward Livvy and Cilla and Brendan. "I'm going to say goodbye to the happy couple," he said.

Sam walked beside him, then suddenly tossed his empty bottle on one of the trays set up in the room. "Talk to you later, Ward. Someone looks like she needs to dance."

Ryan watched as Sam headed toward Julia Carleton like a heat-seeking missile. "Good luck with that, kid," he said, but Sam was long gone. Julia, a detective, kept her personal life very private. Sam might be a hotshot baseball player, but being related to a fellow cop? He didn't stand a chance with Carleton.

To Ryan's surprise, Julia smiled at Sam and headed onto the dance floor with him.

As Ryan stared at the two of them, an arm snaked around his waist. "Livvy," he smiled, turning to kiss his fiancee. "Time to say goodbye to Bren and Cilla?"

"Yeah," she said, leaning up to drag her mouth over his. "Then we have a date to go fishing."

Her eyes were still dark and dilated, and her cheeks were flushed. Seeing how aroused Livvy still was, he stirred again. "Or maybe we should just go home," he murmured.

"Yeah," she said, leaning closer. "Good idea. More...options."

"I like options," he said, his voice low and dark. They stared at each other, exchanging silent promises, until the deejay interrupted.

"Brendan and Cilla are heading out. Let's all say goodbye to them." His amplified voice bounced off the walls, and Livvy took Ryan's hand to lead him toward the crowd.

Ten minutes later, Brendan and Cilla were gone. Still holding hands, Ryan gripped Livvy's hand as they turned at the same time and headed for the exit.

"Great minds," Livvy said with a grin.

Ryan wrapped his arm around Livvy's shoulder, letting his fingers trail over the soft skin of her upper arm. "Faster," he murmured, nipping at her ear. "Before someone else wants to talk."

Five minutes later, they were in Ryan's car, pulling out of the parking lot. "You feel bad about ducking out on everyone?" he asked as he pressed the accelerator.

"Maybe a little," Livvy said, turning in her seat to grin at him. "Not enough to go back, though."

She put her hand on his thigh, drawing tiny circles on his suit pants. Her fingers crept higher and higher, until he grabbed her hand. Removed it from his leg.

"Spoilsport."

"Hey, I want to get home in one piece." He slid his hand through her hair, then drew away reluctantly. "I have lots of options I want to explore."

A half-hour later, he slotted his car into a spot along the curb, then helped Livvy out of the car. His fingers curled around her waist, pulling her against him. The fall air was cool, and her dress left her back and arms exposed.

It only took a couple of minutes to get up the stairs and into their apartment. Pushing the door closed, Ryan engaged the deadbolt, then drew Livvy into his arms.

"Let's get married soon," he whispered, nipping at her neck. "It can be whatever you want, as long as it's soon. No taking a year to plan it, like Cilla did."

"Hmm," she hummed, burrowing beneath his suit jacket. She pulled his shirt out of his pants, then ran her hands up his back. He shivered as she scratched him lightly.

"I think we could do that. But no wedding talk tonight. I have other plans for you." She pressed her mouth to his, and by the time they ran out of air, both of them were trembling.

Livvy cupped his face in both hands. "I love you, Ryan Ward. I can't wait to be married to you." She kissed him again and murmured against his lips, "But right now, take me to bed. Let's go explore our options. All night long."

* * * * *

If you enjoyed **Save Me**, pick up the next book in the series – **See Me**.

177

ABOUT THE AUTHOR

Two-time Rita finalist Margaret Watson published her first book in June, 1991. Since then, she has written thirty books for Silhouette Intimate Moments and Harlequin SuperRomance, as well as nine titles in the Donovan Family series.

Margaret's books have won or been finalists in many contests, including the Colorado Award of Excellence, Desert Rose Golden Quill, Holt Medallion, and National Reader's Choice.

When she's not writing, Margaret practices veterinary medicine. She lives in the Chicago area with her husband, three daughters and a menagerie of pets.

* * *

Thank you for reading Save Me. I'm honored you chose one of my books, and I hope you enjoyed it!

- If you would like to receive an email newsletter when my next book is released, sign up at **www.margaretwatson.com**.
- Reviews help other readers find books they'd like to read. Please leave a review of Love Me at your favorite on-line retailer. I welcome all reviews.
- Please recommend Love Me to your friends and on discussion boards.